"You don't need a wife, Pete."

When he didn't answer, Rachelle persisted, "You haven't any time for one."

He gave a pained smile. "You surprise me," he jeered softly. "I would say we both need marriage."

Rachelle, recalling the many unions they had shared, felt hot color flood her face. "People change, you know," she said in a low voice.

"I wouldn't say you've changed," Pete contradicted. "You still want the best of both worlds."

"Our life together is finished as far as I'm concerned!" she retorted.

Rachelle did not like the strange way he was looking at her. He was far too experienced, too attractive, for her ever to get the better of him. But she had to try. The present situation was impossible—even though she still loved him!

KATRINA BRITT
is also the author of these
Harlequin Romances

and this
Harlequin Presents

Many of these titles are available at your local bookseller.

For a free catalogue listing all available Harlequin Romances and Harlequin Presents, send your name and address to:

HARLEQUIN READER SERVICE
M.P.O. Box 707, Niagara Falls, NY 14302
Canadian address: Stratford, Ontario N5A 6W2

The Wrong Man

by

KATRINA BRITT

Harlequin Books

TORONTO • LONDON • LOS ANGELES • AMSTERDAM
SYDNEY • HAMBURG • PARIS • STOCKHOLM • ATHENS • TOKYO

Original hardcover edition published in 1980
by Mills & Boon Limited

ISBN 0-373-02397-9

Harlequin edition published April 1981

CHAPTER ONE

RACHELLE gave a deep sigh of utter bliss from the depths of the bubble bath. Lovely to be home again, to settle down in her own image with no more soul-searching. Humming a catchy little tune, she lifted a shapely leg and soaped it dreamily with a huge sponge. Looking back, one could say that she had led a charmed life, with tennis courts and riding stables just around the corner from her home in a quiet residential suburban environment.

Most of her friends had been kept from schooldays, boys she had danced with, skied, sailed, and motored with through the years. It would have stayed that way if it had not been for Pete.

In her twenty-fourth year she had been removed from the pivot of her existence by forces beyond her control. Now, two years later, at the age of twenty-six she was back on an even keel. A smile lifted the corners of her mouth. She must have been quite a girl to hook the biggest heart-throb of the moment—or had he hooked her?

Of course he had, delicately, skilfully, masterfully and without mercy. Pete's charms were polished to a nonchalant perfection, dangerously so in the way that it would take some time to recover from the effects.

She was in a white towelling robe, her brown hair coiled in a towel, when her mother entered the room.

Minnie Barclay was a petite five feet and a bit who twittered like a bird with feathers of the expensive down variety. But she always looked so lovely in every-thing she wore that one had to forgive her extra-vagance. She fluttered forward to offer her usual perfumed peck with a delighted smile.

'Lovely to see you, darling,' she cooed, pursing a pretty mouth skilfully made up like the rest of her smooth, almost unlined complexion. Her blonde hair was natural with a few streaks of silver adding instead of detracting from its sheen. 'How long are you propos-ing to stay?'

'Indefinitely.'

Rachelle sat down and proceeded to manicure her nails, and Minnie, tongue in cheek, took in the enchant-ing lines of her daughter's legs revealed through the opening of the white towelling robe right down to the soft fluffy slippers on her slender feet. She had often wondered whether Rachelle knew how she envied her the extra inches that those long lovely legs gave her.

'You don't mean to say you've left Pete for good?' she cried, coming back to the subject in hand. 'I can't believe it!' She lifted delicate hands. 'Why?'

'Because I've had enough of being a termite wallow-ing in mud and oil,' Rachelle answered firmly, then asked affectionately after her mother's health, ending with, 'Where's Grandpa?'

Minnie looked a trifle uncomfortable and sat down on the settee to slip the tiny, beautifully cut shoes from her dainty feet. Her smile was one of blissful relief as she wiggled her toes.

'Grandpa is away, so you can have his room. It's bigger than yours.'

'Away? Grandpa away? He never goes anywhere further than his old crony down the road.' Rachelle paused in her task, orange stick held in mid-air.

'Mother, define "away",' she demanded, her blue eyes apprehensive.

Minnie patted her faultless hair-do uneasily. 'He's ... hmm ... he's taking a rest by the sea.'

'With his crony, Mr Wills?'

'No. You see, there's this very nice home for retired gentlefolk ...'

'Mother, you don't mean...?' Rachelle was beyond words.

'Yes, I do.' Minnie was unperturbed by her daughter's shocked reaction. 'Yes. It was his own idea.'

Rachelle swallowed on a dry throat. 'But why? Grandpa's perfectly sound in wind and limb and he's only in his late sixties. What's been going on?'

'I'd like a cup of tea. What about you?' Minnie said brightly.

Rachelle rose to her feet and walked to the window overlooking the garden. The roses which were the love of her grandfather's life were especially lovely this year. Her blue eyes misted and her face set, then she swung round to follow her mother determinedly to the ultra-modern kitchen where she was switching on the kettle.

Very quietly Rachelle said, 'You didn't ask Grandpa to go because I was coming home, did you? I'm not staying with you—I'm getting a flat of my own in London.'

Minnie set cups and saucers on a tray along with milk, sugar and biscuits before making a reply.

'I'm thinking about giving up this house and moving into a flat myself,' she explained carefully. 'You must have noticed the amount of building going on around here, and we have some very nice flats going up along the road.'

Rachelle said cuttingly, 'The only thing I've noticed is that the nicest member of the family is missing and I want him back. Have your flat if that's what you want, but leave Grandpa his home.'

Her voice trembled a little as her mother calmly warmed the teapot and spooned in the tea.

'And how do you propose that I buy a flat without the money from selling this house?' she asked coolly.

'You have money enough. The suit you're wearing would keep Grandpa for a year, and you know it—and how dare you act without consulting Geoff and me?'

'Geoff is perfectly content to let me decide for myself. After all, I'm not old yet and I have some time before me.'

Rachelle said scathingly, 'Geoff would be. Like you, he's never cared for anyone but himself. Grandpa is entitled to live his life, just as you're entitled to yours.'

Minnie said, 'Would you like coffee or tea?' as she filled the teapot with boiling water, adding as Rachelle shook her head, 'We'll talk it over later. We have to get ready for the party this evening. You know Tony Spelling is coming? There's going to be quite a crowd. Cheer you up.'

She smiled into the blue-shadowed gaze of her daughter as she carried the tray into the lounge and set it down.

Rachelle sat down and accepted her tea. 'I'm glad Tony is coming. It's important that we should settle things about my new appointment now I've finally broken with Pete.'

'But has he broken with you?'

Rachelle all but choked on her tea. 'What do you mean? We've talked it over and there's nothing more to say. Pete was already married to an oil drill before he met me.'

'Pete is here,' said her mother. 'He's coming to the party tonight. I believe he wants to see Tony Spelling. After all, the man is a millionaire.'

Rachelle's colour had gone, but she kept her cool. 'Tony doesn't dabble in oil except where art is concerned. He's a patron of the arts, not a prospector. He's only interested in oil used in paints on canvas.'

'That's as maybe, but he's coming just the same.'

Rachelle's hand trembled as she put down her cup. 'Where is Pete staying?'

'At somebody's penthouse in London. He's gone to see your grandfather.'

Rachelle took a deep breath. There was something she had to make clear.

'Pete and I have parted by mutual consent. I haven't seen him for some time. We just aren't compatible. I mean, I'm Libra and he's Leo, and ... and we just didn't get on.'

Minnie leaned over and patted her hand. 'I know. I do love you, you know, darling, and I understand.'

Rachelle swallowed some more of her tea. 'What did Pete tell you?'

'Nothing. Not a word. I've only had your letters to go on. I don't want to pry, but I never could imagine you in oily overalls and a shiny nose after the way you've been brought up.'

Rachelle lowered her eyes, and fingered her cup. 'It was pigging it, to put it lightly,' she admitted. 'Pete even took his blueprints to bed!'

'He's all man, darling. You have to admit that.' Minnie sighed. 'He's the kind of man I always dreamed about. He did sweep you off your feet and carry you away.'

'To dump me into a puddle of oil,' Rachelle retorted tartly.

Dressing that evening for the party, Rachelle wished she could have been more frank with her mother about Pete. It would have been heaven to break down in the comfort of her arms to sob out how she felt about him, how she missed him at night, how the anger and frustration of the day had been charmed magically away by his lovemaking. Those masculine hands of his had been tender, cupping her face as their lips had met, caressing her gently into a sudden flaring need for his closeness.

Strangely enough she had met him at a party given by her mother.

Minnie had said carelessly, 'He's a kind of engineer, all tanned and sinewy—been round the world— dabbles in oil wells or something. He won't be your cup of tea, darling, since he doesn't dance or play tennis or anything like that. It will only be a courtesy call since Geoff asked him to drop in. I believe he's very quiet, not much for noise. Ella Stokes asked him to her party last week and he didn't say much, just looked around as if he was planning to set an oil drill in the centre of her enormous lounge. It was positively unnerving!'

Rachelle had laughed, then forgot all about him. The party had been in full swing when Rachelle had barged into the very deep voice.

Topping everyone else in the room with the kind of square shoulders that could burst open any door, he had shut everything out.

'Hello,' he said. 'Do you come here often?'

'Not more than all the time. I live here. Where do you live?'

'Somewhere you've probably not heard of—Calgary and thereabouts.'

Rachelle had stared at him and had been the first one to lower her eyes. So he was tough and on the defensive. Well, she could be tough too, having had plenty of experience in freezing off the wolves. Not that he was one. This one had all the appearance of a wolf, since he was much too attractive, with his black hair and clean-shaven long clear-cut features, to lead a celibate life. But he was no ladies' man. He was much, too much, man.

'You've come far enough away. Is someone after you?' she asked sweetly.

'Not that I'm aware of,' said Pete laconically. 'How about you?'

'Me?' Rachelle had been flippant. 'I don't understand.'

He had surveyed her dispassionately. 'Most girls as attractive as you are usually spoken for.'

'I don't live with anyone, nor am I engaged, but that's hardly your business, is it?' she retorted.

She stared up at his mahogany face, at the dark-lashed grey eyes, and had been surprised to discover that there could be nothing more delightful than that he should make it his business. However, while it was clear that he would be exciting to know, Rachelle felt the need to assure him that she was not just a pretty face in search of a husband.

On the contrary, he discovered just that. Frankly she told him how she had changed the secretarial job she had held down for years for one in the beauty business. She had trained hard as a beautician and was now hoping to put two years of college training into practice.

His well-cut mouth had lifted in amusement as he had congratulated her on her endeavours. He had even agreed with her that there was no reason why she should not continue with her job after marriage. That was when he proposed. As he reminded her later, he had not stipulated the time she should work after they were married, although he did understand the need to practise what she had learned in theory while it was still fresh in her mind.

Rachelle had studied hard during her training, ploughing through the medical knowledge necessary, such as knowing the exact area of body muscles during massage. It had been sheer luck for her to secure a post that covered practically every field of her training. After an idyllic honeymoon Rachelle had carried on with her work while Pete was involved in exploratory work in oilfields off the English coast.

As Rachelle's work was in London they had taken a flat there and for twelve months everything had gone well. Then Pete had gone back to oilfields nearer home. He had sold their flat and had taken her back with him. Rachelle, very much in love, had agreed, and had started a beauty parlour near to the place of his work. But it had been a far cry from the kind of thing she was used to in London.

Furthermore, Pete was immersed in his job up to his firm sunburned neck, and Rachelle resented it, resented the stinking oilfields, the dirt, the lack of the higher standard of living she was used to. The end had come when she had lost her baby.

One did not get over a miscarriage so easily, especially when one's husband was taken up with other demanding roles like nursing oil drills, so Rachelle had left.

Pete had been very calm about it. He had spoken quietly with a slight loss of colour. If she walked out on him he was not going to stop her. If that was all her love was worth then there was nothing to keep her with him.

Rachelle's mouth twisted wryly. Her life had gone a complete cycle. She was in the same house, preparing to meet Pete again as if they were the strangers they were at their first meeting. Then her hair had been long and she had done it up in coils on her head. She had created a new image now with her silky locks cut short and allowed to fall into natural shining waves.

Her dainty high-heeled sandals were a must to combat his height, and the lovely shaded pink and purple check dress with its smart stand-up collar and elasticated waist gave her an air of utter sophistication. Minnie thought so too when she came for Rachelle to zip her up into her sheath dress of white brocade shot with a gold thread.

'You look lovely, darling,' she cooed. 'You've certainly not lost that air of sophistication.'

Rachelle said, 'Who did you have to zip you up before? Grandpa?'

Minnie looked embarrassed. 'I miss him,' she admitted. 'Hurry up downstairs, I want to show you off.'

Rachelle waited until most of the guests arrived before going downstairs. Even so some sixth sense told her that Pete had not yet arrived. The lounge was brilliant with colour and sound. Minnie never had distorted music by sheer volume of sound bursting the eardrums at her parties—which was one reason why they were so successful, Rachelle thought. Pete would undoubtedly approve.

She was greeted by warm exclamations of pleasure by old friends and by the time Pete arrived Rachelle was quite prepared to meet him. He was accompanied by Tony Spelling, a wide-shouldered, deep-chested man of medium height, casually dressed, very well groomed with a dark shrewd expression which had relaxed into a smile at something Pete had obviously said. He could charm the devil, Rachelle thought viciously. If he had spoiled her chances she would kill him!

Instantly her eyes met Pete's across the room. His expression startled her ... Sardonic? Malicious? Shrewdly kind? Challenging? It was impossible to know. What did it matter? The important thing was that Tony Spelling was there and he was clearly in a lighthearted mood. That mood, even if temporary, gave her spirits a lift.

Then both men were bearing down upon her, Tony's eyes alight with interest.

Pete said ominously, 'My wife Rachelle. Darling, Tony Spelling.'

Tony smiled at her. 'Pete is a very lucky man,' he murmured as he took her hand. 'Enchanted to meet you, Mrs Standring.'

'Oh, Pete—Mr Spelling,' Minnie beamed, 'please forgive me if I rush you into dinner. The soufflé ...'

Instantly Pete took Minnie's arm and whispered something as they moved to the dining room. The result was that he sat next to Tony Spelling at dinner with Rachelle on Tony's other side.

She ought to have known that Pete would claim Tony's attention all through the meal. It did not help matters that Rachelle's companion on her other side was an old school friend who was determined to put her wise about everything that had happened from the time they last met. The food was delicious. Minnie's old school friend, a Cordon Bleu expert, had prepared it and her son waited on at table.

Immediately afterwards Minnie took Tony Spelling away and Rachelle found herself with Pete. Suddenly she found herself on the cool dark patio with him beside her.

'You did it on purpose, didn't you?' she cried fiercely. 'You knew I wanted to see Tony Spelling and you deliberately kept him from talking to me!'

He eyed her dispassionately. 'Tony Spelling is still here. What are you making a fuss about?'

Rachelle stared at his clear-cut features, teak brown and angled against the light from the windows behind them. Something stirred in her breast and a lump rose in her throat. Flung from a high note of expectancy to bitter disappointment, she drew a deep breath which emerged as a sob. She saw life without Pete stretching out in a never-ending stream of days in which every moment had to be occupied. What did she want, exactly? Suddenly tears blocked her throat, scalded her eyes and fell down her face.

She felt warm hands on her arms guiding her into a dim corner of the patio and a handkerchief was thrust into her hand. Drawing her head against his chest, he moved a hand over her slender back. She felt his warmth, his male fragrance, and the longing to feel the pressure of his lips on hers was almost too much.

'Now, now,' he murmured. 'If meeting Tony Spelling means that much to you ...'

Rachelle stiffened. 'What makes you think I'm ... crying ... for Tony Spelling?' she cried.

'It's only natural that you should feel scared and insecure now that you're joining the ranks of the marriage failures. I can understand how you feel.'

Rachelle sniffed into his handkerchief and pushed him away.

'It wasn't that at all ... it was ... it was ...'

'Yes?'

Rachelle gulped and pulled herself up short. What an idiot she was! A moment more in his arms and she would have been sobbing out her love for him.

'It's Grandpa,' she gasped, and the tears came again.

'Ah yes. I believe you have his room. Very convenient for you, his going away?'

She glared at him with tear-wet eyes. 'I knew nothing about it. You ... you don't think I had anything to do with him going away, do you?'

She watched his clear-cut mouth thin suddenly. 'I don't know. All I know is that he's having his room back tonight.'

'Tonight?' Rachelle echoed.

'Yes. You're going with me to the flat I have in London. We have things to talk over.'

Rachelle drew a deep breath of indignation and snapped her fingers.

'Just like that?' she cried. 'Who do you think you are, giving me orders?'

'I'm your husband ... yet,' he told her with a set face.

'Thanks for that encouraging last word! Now you can get out of my way. I'm going to see Tony Spelling to ask for a chance to qualify for a job in the new art centre he's financing.'

Pete caught her wrist and she was reminded of his strength. Her blue eyes stabbed him with anger and she tried in vain to loosen his grip.

'You can see Tony later. First of all you're going to pack your bags,' he said.

'Let go my wrist, you brute! You're hurting me!' she cried.

'You're hurting yourself. Come on—first we're going to your room and you're moving out.'

'And if I refuse?' Rachelle lifted her chin defiantly.

He eyed her dispassionately. 'Don't make me despise you more than I already do. Come on.'

But Rachelle refused to move, and he looked at her for a long moment. Then he spoke again.

'I said don't make me despise you more than I do already,' he repeated.

She stopped struggling and stared at him curiously. 'That makes two of us. Why should you despise me?'

'Because you're a hypocrite.'

Rachelle continued to stare at him. Her worst enemy could never have accused her of hypocrisy or dishonesty. The only depths in her were depths of character, the courage to believe in her own convictions. Her only weakness, if one could call it so, was that she was inclined on occasions to allow her heart to rule her head.

Her hand came up to strike his face even before she herself was aware of it. Pete did not flinch, but his mouth tightened as the slap on his brown cheek reverberated like a pistol shot on the night air. His instant reaction was to put her arm behind her back and haul her against him. Then he pulled back her head by her hair and brought down his face near to her own.

'Do that again,' he warned, 'and you'll be sorry! I can retaliate in a way you won't like. You get my meaning? Now move!'

He released her sharply and she swayed for a moment in regaining her balance. Her face was a luminous pearl, her blue eyes deep pools of emotion. She did not move and continued to stare up at him as one hypnotised. Her lips hardly moved.

'I want to know why you called me a hypocrite,' she insisted.

'Well, aren't you? You profess to love your grand-father, yet you can take over his room without the slightest compunction knowing that he's in a home,' he answered darkly.

'But I haven't ... I didn't ...' Rachelle stammered in confusion.

'Then why are you refusing to move out?'

She closed her eyes to squeeze the tears behind them. Then very slowly she turned on her heel and Pete followed her. She had taken her clothes from the wardrobe and put them in her suitcase, and was taking exquisite underwear from drawers when she was aware of him watching her from the doorway.

The heat rose in her cheeks as he watched her fold the delicate garments. His smile was meaningful, mocking, and slightly malicious.

'I trust your perfume doesn't linger until your grandfather arrives like it did at the bungalow after you left. It haunts me still,' he jeered.

Rachelle closed her suitcase mechanically and stared at his brown mocking face.

Her voice came in a choked whisper. 'Did you say ... Grandpa's coming home?'

He grinned. 'He's next door with Mr Wills. I took him with me to the home to persuade your grandfather to come back. It seems he went of his own accord when Minnie told him about wanting to sell the house and move into a flat ... Hey, where are you going?'

His last words fell on empty air, for Rachelle had gone like the wind, knocking against him in the pro-cess. It was a few moments before he moved to pick up her case and carry it slowly from the room. It was just as well that Rachelle did not see the expression on his face. Those steps of hers would not have been half so light if she had.

It was some time later when Pete strolled down the road to meet them. It was a transformed Rachelle who linked her grandfather's arm while she looked up at him adoringly. Pete walked with them, his arm loosely draped around the elderly man's shoulders.

'That was some shock we had to find you gone, old-timer,' he said teasingly. 'Don't do it again, will you?'

Rachelle followed his lead. 'It wasn't a bit like home without you, Grandpa. You know Mother—she's a bit featherbrained, but she means well, and she would never willingly hurt you.'

Sam Rodson's smile included them both. 'Bless you both,' he said paternally. 'I just can't believe it. You know what?'

They both looked at him in what seemed to be a very moving moment.

Sam spoke each word with relish. 'I've just beat Ben Wills at chess and he's no mean hand at it. It's made my day!'

Rachelle broke into helpless giggles with the warm air of her laughter drying the tears trembling on her lashes.

'Grandpa,' she gasped, convulsed, 'you're so sane, so uncomplicated ... I love you.'

She reached up to kiss his cheek with Pete's intent gaze focussed upon her.

He drawled, 'Good for you. Shows you haven't lost your touch. What about coming to stay with Rachelle and me at our flat in London? Plenty of room, and you need the break. Ben is going to take some time to recover from his defeat and you have to prepare yourself to do battle for the next contest.'

Sam's eyes twinkled. 'An invitation from two of my favourite people,' he said. 'I'll think about it. And thanks, Pete ... thanks a lot.'

CHAPTER TWO

THEY were on their way to the flat and Rachelle awoke as Pete braked. Her head had fallen against his shoulder and she sat up blinking sleepily.

'We've arrived,' he told her coolly. 'You can unlock the door while I get your suitcase from the trunk.'

Rachelle took the key and stared with wide eyes at the familiar façade of flats in her favourite part of Chelsea. Then she was looking down at the key in her hand before raising her eyes to his dark face.

'You don't mean to say ...?' she began.

He nodded. 'The very same flat that we had before. Yes.'

'But ... but we sold it?'

'That's right, to an old friend of mine. It's ours for as long as we want it.'

The brittle smile hid her dismay. Pete was not exactly playing fair to expect her to return to a place where they had known such happiness.

Her shrug was one of acceptance. 'Ah well,' she said resignedly, 'it won't be for long, will it? Once I've seen Tony Spelling and we've had a talk, I'll be moving out. I wouldn't want to put you out.'

'You won't,' he assured her dryly. 'Now open the door, there's a good girl.'

His offhandedness annoyed her, but she obeyed,

opening the door and switching on the lights to strange furnishings. Then Pete was striding in with her suitcase.

'I'm putting you into the master bedroom,' he announced, and was about to do just that when Rachelle put a hand on his arm.

Her face was suffused with colour. She cried hotly, 'If you think I'm going to share your bed . . .'

His look cut her down to size. 'Pipe down! I'm in one of the guest rooms—more to my bachelor taste and state.'

Feeling rather foolish, Rachelle wondered what she was doing there at all. It would have been easy enough to insist upon staying at home in the smaller spare room, but she did not want her grandfather to feel that he was putting her out.

The flat was spotless and beautifully furnished. The kitchen sparkled with the latest gadgets—no dirty dishes around. Reaching for a shining pan, Rachelle tipped milk into it and turned on the cooker. She was filling two cups with a bedtime drink when Pete strolled into the lounge.

She called, 'There's a drink here for you. I'm taking mine to bed.'

He did not reply, did not even turn his head as she went through the lounge on the way to her room.

She was at the door when he said, 'Thanks. Goodnight.'

Rachelle paused, said quietly, 'I want to thank you for what you've done for Grandpa today. I'm very . . .'

'Go to bed,' he growled, presenting the back of wide shoulders and a well-shaped head.

She stiffened, finding his back view distinctly irritating. Why on earth didn't he turn round? He might have been sorting his mail, but it was no excuse for rudeness.

She went on doggedly, 'I don't want you to have a distorted view of Mother. She's sweet really and intelligent, although she gives the impression sometimes of being scatty. There isn't a malicious bone in her body, which is why ... Daddy ... we all love her so much.'

'For God's sake go to bed,' Pete repeated.

Rachelle awoke after a night of unbroken sleep to a sunny welcome. Rays of warmth were stealing between the Venetian blinds across the room. The king-size bed, a collection of muted colours to match the lovely pale room, the soft fondant-coloured rugs and eau-de-nil furniture which one dreamed about but only a big cheque book could buy, filled her with a kind of sybaritic bliss.

The bathroom was no less enchanting when she padded into it on deep-pile carpet. The fittings were the same as she remembered, but the glass shelves were filled with expensive jars and the towel rails covered in luxuriously thick soft fluffy towels.

A far cry from the bungalow at the oilfields, she thought with a sigh. Rachelle was not really mercenary, but she did reckon that there was more to life than spending the best years of one's life pigging it out in dust and dirt. Pete did not share her views. He was happy enough to make a break once in a while away from it all, then was all the more eager to go back.

She washed, dressed and unpacked her clothes, consoling herself that they would not be there for long. The soft green tailored blouse and matching fine check slacks brought out the amber glow in her brown locks.

She looked slender and willowy and without a care in the world.

The kitchen was impregnated with the delicious aroma of coffee and there was corn on the cob, highly seasoned and yellow with butter.

'Good morning,' said Pete with quizzical dents at the corners of his mouth. 'Sleep well?'

'Lovely. Did you?'

He pulled out her chair. 'My sleep these days is a trifle haunted, but I'm getting used to it. Cereal or fruit juice?'

Rachelle sat down and lifted her eyes to his dark face.

'Fruit juice, please,' she answered, marvelling as she had always done at his capacity for good grooming. His dark hair was neatly trimmed, his tanned face smooth and smelling discreetly of aftershave, and his hands were well cared for. No one would ever guess what his job entailed. The oil and dirt was in another world.

'Why so quiet?' he asked, sitting down opposite to her at the table.

She smiled. 'The strangeness of it all, I suppose. Yesterday I was beginning another life—away from you, doing my own thing.'

'And now?' he queried.

'Back at square one, aren't we?'

He tucked into his cereal. 'Not necessarily,' he said equably. 'I've made an appointment for you with Tony Spelling for lunch today.'

Rachelle almost choked on her fruit juice. 'You have?'

He nodded. 'That's what you wanted, isn't it?'

'Oh yes ... of course ... What time?'

'He's picking you up here at twelve-thirty.'

Rachelle rose from her chair with her empty glass.

'You're quiet again,' Pete mused as she put bread into the toaster. 'Why not have some cereal? Toast is no good to start the day on.'

'Why not get on with your own breakfast and leave me to mine?' she said tartly.

'Now you're angry. I wonder why? Didn't you want to see Tony Spelling after all?'

Rachelle sat down and waited for the toast. She said snappishly, 'You don't have to butt in. I was going to make an appointment with Tony myself. I hope you didn't say anything about ... us ... you and me, I mean.'

He leaned back on the two back legs of his chair with his cup of coffee and eyed her tongue in cheek.

'I did have to explain a little why you wanted a date with him, otherwise he would have thought it somewhat strange,' he replied sardonically. 'I told him briefly all about this very intensive training you had and how you want to put it into practice in case you lost it.'

'Very touching!' Rachelle took the popped-up toast and buttered it liberally. 'If you ruin my chances I'll ...'

'Yes?' Pete raised a provocative brow.

'Forget it,' she snapped.

'I'm glad you aren't threatening me,' he told her softly, dangerously. 'And it is a job you're after, isn't it?'

Her cheeks darkened with anger. 'And what do you mean by that?' she stormed.

'Tony is a millionaire and not too old.'

'Charming!' Her small teeth crunched into the toast, and she tried to keep her feelings in check. 'What makes you think I would go after another man?'

'I'm not thinking anything. Women have a leaning towards millionaires.'

Pete sounded decidedly bored and Rachelle could cheerfully have hit him. Yet her temper was muted by the thought that it was bitter-sweet to be having breakfast with him again, to have him giving her his attention instead of rushing off to his work. She felt her heartbeats quicken and she took her time over her breakfast, not wanting it to end. Pete helped himself to more coffee and replenished her cup with his eyes on her face.

She smiled at him, not wanting the feeling of belonging to melt away into thin air. Pete lighted a cigarette and surveyed her with narrowed eyes.

'What would you say to your grandfather spending a few days with us? He hasn't seen much of London.'

Rachelle swallowed the last morsel of toast. 'Why exactly are you here, Pete?' she asked.

'To get Tony Spelling interested in my scheme. I need a good backer. Why?'

Rachelle met his intent gaze over her coffee cup. 'Your work means everything to you, doesn't it?'

He blew a line of smoke towards the ceiling. 'I wouldn't say that.'

'I would,' Rachelle persisted. 'You don't need a wife. You haven't any time for one.'

He gave a pained smile. 'You surprise me,' he jeered softly. 'I would say we both need marriage.'

Rachelle, recalling the reunions they had shared, felt the hot colour flood her face.

'People change, you know,' she said low-voiced.

'I wouldn't say you've changed,' he contradicted. 'You still want the best of both worlds.'

'I don't think that's fair,' she protested, putting

down her cup with some heat. Did he have to be so uncaring, so superior? 'Men always see things from their own viewpoint.'

'They have to do today, what with Women's Lib and all that nonsense. And if you're hankering after a divorce, it's not on.'

Rachelle's nostrils quivered. In vain she sought to play it cool with the knowledge that he was deliberately provoking her. Losing her control meant that she would be playing into his hands. Looking at his lean, mocking face, she was shaken into an emotion which she was too angry to analyse. Normally she was not given to fits of rage or even losing her temper so fiercely.

'Fortunately it won't be left to you,' she retorted. 'Our life together is finished as far as I'm concerned. I'm all out for the career I was embarking upon when we met. So will you please leave me alone.'

'But you're wrong, my sweet. We had a row and off you went, knowing I couldn't follow at the time.'

Rachelle jumped to her feet. 'Our parting was final, so why won't you accept it?' she cried.

'People say things in the heat of the moment that they afterwards regret,' he reminded her. 'Why did you run away?'

Rachelle was leaving the room tightlipped when he grasped her shoulders.

'I'm talking to you. Please answer my question.'

'You know why I went. You would have won me over like you always did.' She eyed him defiantly. 'You'll notice that I used the past tense.'

'You mean I couldn't win you over now ... if I chose?' His tones were dangerously soft and she quivered. 'Don't tempt me,' he continued. 'The chemistry between us is pretty powerful.'

'You knew that, didn't you?' she cried. 'You think it's still as strong as ever. Well, you're wrong!'

'You're living dangerously, my sweet.' He smiled reminiscently. 'Want me to prove it?'

'There, you see! You ... you don't play the game ... you take advantage because of your beastly physical attractions ...'

His hold on her shoulders slackened. 'I'm sorry you feel like that. You've changed if you're mistaking lust for love.'

Rachelle did not like the way he was looking at her, as if he was seeing her with different eyes. She couldn't say anything without being perilously near to tears. She had fooled herself that Pete meant nothing to her any more, only to discover that she was as madly in love with him as she had ever been.

But what about him? Not only had he found her weak spot, her love for him, he also had an uncanny perception as to what her reaction would be to his every move. He was far too experienced, too everything, for her ever to have the better of him. But she had to try. The situation as it was shattered her by its impossibility.

The shrill ring of the telephone cut in on her unhappy thoughts. Pete released her and answered it. Five minutes later he had left the flat.

Tony Spelling was smiling at Rachelle across the luncheon table. 'I'm giving a party this evening, Mrs Standring, and it will give me great pleasure if you and your husband will come. I'm giving it at the hotel where I'm staying—your husband knows where it is.'

Rachelle returned his smile uncertainly. He had

brought her to his club for a wonderful lunch, listened attentively to her replies as he questioned her as to her experience as a beautician and had promised to consider her in his plans for a precinct of art culture. Furthermore, she liked him.

She searched for the right words. 'I'm sorry I can't answer you right away regarding my husband. I ... I have no idea if he has anything planned for this evening. I'll ask him to telephone you.'

Rachelle filled in the afternoon shopping and having tea, returning to the flat in the late afternoon. As she let herself in she heard Pete speaking in the lounge. He was on the telephone, having discarded his jacket and tie. His shirt neck was open, showing a well developed chest, hirsute and dark. He had dropped into a chair with the receiver in his hand and one long leg was slung over the chair arm. He looked big and uncaring and heartbreakingly attractive.

Rachelle hesitated in the doorway with her parcels and waited.

'Hello,' he said, putting down the telephone. 'Have a nice lunch?'

He looked tired yet insolent, in a mood that she hated.

'Tony is giving a party this evening at his hotel and he wants us to go. I told him you'd telephone him.'

'Want to go?' he asked casually.

'It's up to you,' she replied, borrowing his coolness.

He took his time looking her trim figure over. 'How did the interview go?' he asked.

'He's going to consider me.'

'The job means a lot to you, does it?' he asked.

She shrugged. 'Of course. I like it.'

Conscious that he was returning her regard with a

cool appraisal that was a kind of rudeness, Rachelle was filled with a vague hostility and something else that confused and disturbed her. She tilted her chin defiantly and as though he sensed it and despised her for it, Pete's face took on a sudden harshness.

Difficult to forget that those long-fingered brown hands had once been so gentle in their caresses. She dragged herself with a jerk from the bitter-sweetness of the tormenting past. Her eyes had an angry darkness as she waited for him to speak.

'What time is this party?' he asked.

'You're supposed to telephone Tony.' Rachelle bit her lip. She did not want to go with him, did not want to share his car or be indebted to him in any way, so she added uncertainly, with a cool little edge to her voice, 'I'm not keen really for you to go if it ... puts you out in any way, I mean. If you have a date already ...'

She stopped, knowing she was babbling. There was an instantaneous setting of his features.

'If you mean have I a date with some luscious blonde ... no, I haven't. I haven't taken to sleeping around either ... yet.'

His tone was almost unbearably hostile and insolent, and Rachelle retreated, a little crimson-faced.

'I didn't mean ...' she began. Her air of dignity sat well on her slender shoulders. 'What I meant was that I could go alone to Tony's party ... I wasn't trying to pry either.'

'Sensible. What I do is really nobody's business but my own. I'll telephone Tony.' Pete reached for the telephone.

It was a very quiet and subdued Rachelle who sat beside Pete in his car on the way to the party. She had

dressed for it feeling terribly nervous. Arriving anywhere with Pete meant that she had to act as his wife.
This posed a special hazard since she could not entirely
relax and pretend to be happy. When they were alone
there were only the few basic polite phrases tossed between them, but in company it was quite different.

Abstractedly, Rachelle wondered what on earth she
was doing with Pete in the first place.

'Delighted to see you,' Tony said heartily when
they arrived, and Rachelle smiled brilliantly too, her
hand lightly on Pete's arm.

The music was not ear-splitting, the food delicious,
the wine perfection and the staff solicitous. Later there
was dancing, and Rachelle took good care to keep away
from Pete.

It did not take much effort on her part, since partners were there without her seeking them. Pete was
talking to Tony for most of the evening, then Tony
asked her for a dance.

For a broad-shouldered stocky man, he was remarkably light on his feet and a good dancer. Rachelle began to enjoy herself and he left her laughing and
breathless.

'I enjoyed that very much,' he told her with a
twinkle in his eyes. 'You dance divinely, Mrs Standring.'

'Call me Rachelle,' she cooed, catching Pete's eye
across the room.

'Then you must call me Tony,' he insisted. 'And
now excuse me. I must see to my other guests. Perhaps
we can dance together later?'

'I'd like that,' she said.

Pete was making his way across the room to her
when someone claimed her for the next dance. She was

circling the room when she saw him talking again to Tony and hoped he wasn't trying to put a spoke in the wheel regarding her own chances of a job. The evening had not been as bad as she had expected.

The main reason had been that she had been able to keep her distance with Pete during the dancing. She had deliberately ignored him twice as he had crossed the room, presumably to dance with her, by dancing off with someone else. It was silly really, but Rachelle knew that she did not want his arms around her. There was only one way to get the better of him—by coolly mustering her own defences. Why did he reduce her to a puppet with no mind of her own?

She felt sick to know that her face betrayed her too easily to Pete's experienced eyes. He had known her too intimately not to recognise her immediate retreat to panic stations where his presence was concerned.

So it was, as the evening wore on, there came a time when it was no longer possible to avoid him. His hand was on her arm and she looked at him quickly, feeling fairly secure in the shadowy light.

'Hello,' she said lightly. 'Lovely party.'

He said tightly, 'Stop trying to impress on me that you're enjoying yourself. And stop behaving as if I put the fear of God into you, do you hear?'

His grip on her arm had tightened painfully as he guided her from the dance floor.

'You're hurting my arm,' she whispered fiercely. 'And I'm not frightened of you!'

'Oh yes, you are,' he said darkly. 'I'm giving you a warning, my sweet. Stop behaving as though I'm the big bad wolf or I'll give you reason to be afraid of me. Do you understand?'

They were so close she felt the warmth of him, saw

the tightening of his jaw as he glared down at her. Not knowing what to expect from anger that she had unwittingly started, she tried to free herself.

He was too strong for her. 'I'm making a telephone call, then I'm coming back, and you will behave like my wife instead of behaving like a giddy teenager with all and sundry.'

He left her sitting at a table and the next moment Tony was there.

'All alone?' he asked.

Rachelle pulled herself together. 'Pete is coming back,' she told him with a smile.

'Can I get you a drink?' he asked. 'You look a little pale.'

'The dancing—it makes you warm.'

'True,' he agreed. 'See you later, then.'

Rachelle bit hard on her lip. 'Tony,' she said as he turned away, 'would you mind if I went home? I have a headache and I think it best for me to go.'

He looked at her curiously. 'Sure you won't have a brandy or something first?'

'No, thanks. I'll find Pete.'

Rachelle knew that Tony was a little curious. What did it matter if he was? He could probably put it down to a little misunderstanding between husband and wife. In two minutes she had been to the cloakroom for her wrap and was outside in a taxi.

By the time she reached the flat she had made up her mind to look for her own accommodation the following morning. She might be lucky and land a decent job. She could go to the place where she had worked after leaving the training college. They might be able to help her.

She heard Pete come in not long after she had got

into bed. The noise of water running through the pipes told her that he was in the bathroom, then she heard a dull thud as if he had fallen or knocked something down. Propping herself up on an elbow, she listened with a loudly beating heart. It could not be an intruder, surely?

She switched on her light and her breath came in short gasps. When the door began to open she hardly knew what to expect.

Pete was staring at her. 'Hell,' he exclaimed, 'don't look so terrified!' He was carrying a cup of steaming liquid. 'I've brought you a hot drink. Tony said you had a bad head. Here's two aspirin.'

The relief was so great as to send her almost hysterical.

'When I heard you moving about, I thought . . . it . . . it was someone breaking in.'

'I suppose you could call me an intruder. Sorry I frightened you,' he apologised, softening a little.

Rachelle sobered and wiped the tears from her eyes in a childish gesture with the tips of her fingers. Then she sat up in bed, aware of her state of undress, and drew up the sheet.

The gesture did not escape him and his smile was not pleasant to see. His face hardened, so did his voice.

'Considering the many hours we've spent in each other's arms without a stitch between us, your modesty is touching. You have nothing to fear from me. It wasn't necessary to invent a headache. I liked you better as you were, complaining about your role as the wife of an oil prospector. At least you were honest.'

He put the drink along with the aspirin on the bedside table, then strode to the door, where he paused.

'I might have known anyone like you would be too

good to be true,' he continued in acid tones. 'Heaven preserve me from the wiles of exquisite-looking creatures in the future! They have nothing apart from their looks to offer.'

Rachelle flinched as he closed the door behind him and flinched again at the closing of his own door. Gone was her fear of possible intruders and in its place was the awful truth that Pete no longer loved her. She was shattered.

Rachelle stepped from the bath and towelled herself dry with one ear strained for sounds of movement in the flat. There were none. Slipping on a wrap, she went into the kitchen to find it empty. No fragrant scent of coffee was in the least detectable and she went into the lounge, then crept to Pete's bedroom to find the door ajar, the room empty.

It was with a sense of relief that she prepared and ate her breakfast. Where Pete was she had no idea, neither did she care. At least it gave her a break to sort out her own affairs and get down to the business of finding somewhere to live.

Her first move was to telephone her old place of employment, but she learned on doing so that two of her former colleagues were away on holiday. No, they didn't need temporary help at the moment; there was enough aid coming from students eager to try their skills while working for degrees. Did she want to leave a message?

'No, thanks. I'll be in touch later when the rest of the staff return,' she said. 'Actually, I'm after living accommodation, a small flat just for one.'

The reply was uncompromising, but her present address was requested in case they wished to contact her.

Rachelle spelt it out, thanked the voice and put the telephone down, to see Pete lolling in the doorway.

'Sorry,' he drawled, 'but you won't be going anywhere. You'll be staying right here.'

'What do you mean?' she whispered above the loud beating of her heart.

'What I say. Your grandfather is coming to stay with us and he has to be kept happy while he's here. We can only do that by burying our differences for the moment and being a normal married couple.'

Rachelle clenched her hands into tight knots. 'You've done this on purpose, haven't you? What have you got against my having a flat of my own?'

'Nothing, nothing at all. You admit to thinking a lot of your grandfather, so now's the time to prove it. He needs a change, to feel wanted. We're going to give him a good time.'

'Is Mother coming too?'

'No.' His tone was derisive as though he was laughing at her. 'I'm going to fetch him this morning—and don't deceive yourself into thinking that his presence here will make any difference to our relationship. All you have to do is behave normally.'

For a moment Rachelle was nonplussed. This unexpected move of his had her all mixed up. Then anger mixed with pride came to her rescue. She would show him!

'Suppose I go to stay with Mother and leave you to entertain Grandpa? I didn't want to come here in the first place. You made me come.'

He raised a provocative dark brow. 'And upset your grandfather, the one you love so much? What do you think he'll say when he finds out you've gone home to your mother while he's here? I'm not having him upset. You understand?'

The heat of anger rising in her throat added a huskiness to her voice.

'Stop threatening me!' she exclaimed. 'I'm not here to do your bidding. I love Grandpa and I won't have him used as a weapon against me.'

His eyes narrowed sternly. 'Why not stop thinking of yourself and think of others for a change? You don't know what love is.' He consulted his wrist watch. 'Time I left. I have a daily woman who comes in to do the housework and the cooking, but I shall expect you to be in this evening with a meal waiting. Your grand-father is having my room.'

A tremor ran through her. That potent charm of his and the lazy narrow-eyed way he was regarding her filled her with foreboding. How long could she hold out against him if ... She had to ask the question as steadily as she could.

'Where are you sleeping. You could share my room with Grandpa and I could have yours. We only have two rooms,' she said.

Pete looked at her speculatively and said with im-personal crispness, 'Your grandfather will want his own room. How do you think he'll feel if he knows we're putting ourselves out for him? He has to feel wanted and not in the way. I want him to feel that the room will be his any time he wants to come here.'

CHAPTER THREE

RACHELLE had filled the flat with soft lights, sweet music and the aroma of an appetising meal when Pete arrived with her grandfather.

'Lovely to have you with us, darling,' she cried, kissing his cheek. 'Come on, sit down. You look tired. What about a drink?'

When Pete came into the lounge after taking their guest's suitcase to his room, she said, 'A drink, darling?'

Carefully she avoided touching his fingers as she gave him his drink.

'Thanks, my sweet.' Pete bent to plant a lazy kiss on her neck, then dropped down beside Sam on the settee and stretched out long legs. 'Good to be back,' he said, and reached out a hand to cover Sam's, adding solicitously, 'Not too tired, are you, sir?'

Sam lowered his glass. His smile included them both. 'No, I'm enjoying it. Your mother sends her love, Rachelle, and hopes to see you when she can.'

Rachelle paused on her way to the kitchen to serve up the meal. She said, 'I'll telephone her later.'

In spite of the tension between her and Pete, Rachelle was surprised at the relaxed atmosphere at the dining table throughout the meal. Conversation was casual, easy and interesting, and Sam looked happy and content.

They had their coffee seated in comfortable chairs in the lounge and the room was impregnated with the aroma of cheroots as the two men smoked to their hearts' content.

'Long time since I had a cheroot as good as this, Pete,' Sam remarked, eyeing the red tip with a smile.

Pete grinned, something that Rachelle, seated on the rug at her grandfather's feet, ignored.

'I've put you a box in your room,' he said. 'A good thing is worth having. I hope you enjoy them.'

Time went on. Pete put on some music and Rachelle made a warm bedtime drink. Sam was beginning to look tired and went to bed after taking his warm drink. Rachelle, careful to avoid a tête-à-tête with Pete, went into the kitchen to wash the dishes. He did not offer to help but sat reading one of the daily newspapers.

'I don't know what you've fixed up for yourself in the matter of sleeping arrangements, but I'm going to bed,' she told him when she returned to the lounge, her task done.

He gave her a cursory glance. 'I can hardly fix up a bed here in the lounge in case your grandfather gets up in the night. I'll make up a bed on the floor in your room.'

Rachelle stared at him in dismay. Was he laughing at her? It was either that or at some secret thought as, throwing down the newspaper, he rose lazily to his feet to take her arm.

Rachelle's heart was beating suffocatingly in her throat, but the need to put on a brave front forced up her chin militantly, and she eyed him defiantly. He met her wide eyes with a steely regard and said lazily,

'You're wondering what devilry I have in mind, aren't you? After all, I am your husband and am quite within my rights if I share your bed, but I've no hankering to take anything that isn't freely given.

What's more, your grandfather comes first at the moment. I will not have him upset in any way by thinking that all isn't well between us. Understand?'

Rachelle stared hard at his dark face. Her tone was contemptuous.

'It seems to me,' she said bitingly, 'that you've brought Grandpa here for your own ends. That being so, I don't have to play along with you if I don't want to.'

Pete pushed her through the doorway of the bedroom, followed her and closed the door behind them. Leaning against it, he looked down on her unmoved.

'You will play along with me whether you want to or not. If you don't I can put a spoke in your wheel regarding your hopes of a job in the Tony Spelling concern. It's up to you. I'm going to make a bed on the floor.'

Her look of contempt deepened, and she looked at him as if he was out of his mind. There was a hint of horror also in her expression as she realised how weak she could become under his cynical battery of charm. Her only weapon against him was anger, and a sense of injustice. In a cool little voice she said,

'Since you're forcing your presence upon me I have no other option—only I'm warning you, don't try any tricks or I'll yell for Grandpa.'

But she was talking to the empty air. Pete had gone to fetch bed linen. Rachelle stalked angrily to the bathroom to clean her teeth. Who did he think he was? As for yelling for her grandfather, it was doubtful whether he would take her part against Pete; he was as much under Pete's spell as she was herself. It was only too easy to imagine him reminding her that Pete was her husband. With an air of frustration Rachelle pushed a heavy wad of hair from her bemused forehead.

Pete had not come back when she returned to the bedroom, so she undressed quickly and slid into bed after turning out the light. Pete came in soon after and made up his bed on the floor. Then all was quiet and she fell asleep.

The appetising aroma of bacon and eggs greeted Rachelle when she went into the kitchen next morning to find her grandfather enjoying his breakfast.

'Good morning, darling,' she said, saluting him on his weatherbeaten cheek with a warm kiss. 'Where's Pete?'

'Gone to fetch the newspapers.' Sam forked up a piece of egg. 'Pete's a good cook. This is delicious.'

He conveyed the egg to a very willing mouth with some satisfaction as Rachelle brought fruit juice from the refrigerator. She let this remark pass, asked if he had enjoyed a good night's sleep and sipped her fruit juice with her blue eyes on his pleasant face.

They were talking and laughing together when Pete returned, to toss a small packet to the old man before putting a sheaf of newspapers on the table.

Rachelle looked on curiously as Sam put the tiny packet in his pocket. Pete had evidently paid a visit to the pharmacist.

'Indigestion pills, Grandpa?' she asked, buttering a slice of toast.

Pete said, 'That's right. Sleep well, my sweet? You did quite a bit of tossing and turning during the night. I expected you to lie in this morning.'

'I have,' she answered pertly. 'It's getting on for ten o'clock. I never heard you get up.'

He kissed the side of her neck. 'I hope you're having more than toast this morning. There's enough for two keeping warm.'

Rachelle recoiled inwardly at the touch of cool lips on her skin. He had brought in the breath of cold morning air. He had shaved and was dressed casually, with the air of making anything he wore seemed correct.

'You know I never eat much breakfast, darling,' she cooed. 'You can make a pig of yourself and eat my share.'

Sam said sternly, 'That's no way to speak to your husband when he's cooked the breakfast, my dear. He's right, you know, you do need more than toast to begin your day.'

He eyed her beautifully proportioned figure with twinkling eyes, finding it impossible to be stern with his delightful granddaughter.

She said pertly, 'If Pete needs more to cuddle he should have married a heavyweight.' She giggled. 'There's one at the drilling fields with beautiful big breasts.' Her eyes glowed impishly as Pete brought in his breakfast to set it on the table. 'Nancy Bigland. How is she, Pete?'

He set his breakfast down on the table without looking up and replied coolly, 'Still brightening the landscape.'

'Filling it would be more like it,' Rachelle murmured, with the voluptuous figure of Nancy in mind. 'What have you in mind for today?'

Pete sat down and began his breakfast. 'Your grandfather and I are going out for the day,' he stated coolly.

Rachelle picked up her cup of tea with dainty hands after refilling her grandfather's cup and her own.

'You don't want me with you?' she queried on a note of surprise.

'Not today,' Pete replied. 'Why not spend the day with your mother? Go shopping or something?'

Rachelle did not answer. Sam had already opened one of the newspapers and Pete would soon be following suit. Rachelle collected the used dishes and carried them to the sink, then went to collect those dishes used by her grandfather. Meeting his calm smile, she returned it in the same vein. No harm in letting him live in a romantic dream for a little while longer, she thought.

Mrs Carne, the daily woman who kept the flat in spick and span order, looked a sprightly fifty, but was in her sixties.

'I don't need the work,' she admitted with bright tones. 'I have a lovely bungalow at Surbiton, but I can't stand it without going out to work since I lost my husband four years ago.'

Rachelle had been around the shops and had returned to the hum of the Hoover cleaner. Now they were enjoying a cup of mid-morning coffee together.

Rachelle offered biscuits. 'You certainly keep the flat spotless,' she said with a warm smile.

Mrs Carne smiled, well pleased. Then she frowned thoughtfully.

'There were some blankets and pillows put in the airing cupboard this morning. They'd been used. Do you want me to send them to the laundry?'

Rachelle had an instant vision of Pete collecting up the things he had used for the night and pushing them back into the airing cupboard.

She said hastily, 'We put friends up for the night and they might come again, so I'd leave them for the moment.'

Mrs Carne nodded comprehendingly. 'Nice husband you have, Mrs Standring. Makes me wish I was your age again. He said the elderly gentleman was in the spare room.'

Rachelle explained laconically, 'My grandfather. He's staying with us for the time being. He's very tidy and considerate. You'll like him.'

'I'm sure I shall. Will there be anything you want in the way of cooking a meal?'

'No, thanks. I can cope.'

Tony Spelling telephoned at midday to ask if she was engaged for the afternoon. If not he would appreciate her going with him to the site of the building project. He was sure she would find the whole block fascinating to review.

Rachelle accepted joyfully with the feeling that life did have its good points sometimes. She spent a pleasant afternoon going around partly finished buildings and giving her own ideas about the site for the beauty parlour.

'You've given me some sound advice about this scheme of mine,' he told her as he returned her to the flat. 'I wonder if you would dine with me this evening and meet my fellow promoters in this scheme. It's my baby, but they had a say in things.'

'I'd be delighted,' she answered.

Rachelle prepared the evening meal, then changed for her date with Tony. Pete and her grandfather arrived just as she was about to leave. Pete let his intelligent grey eyes rove over the picture she made with her bare shoulders gleaming like a pearl through the gossamer wrap, her delicately made up face evanescent as a rose.

'Sorry—must dash,' she cried breathlessly. 'Dinner is all ready. See you later!'

From Rachelle's point of view the evening was not a

success. She was haunted by Pete's face, his grey eyes pale against the deep bronze of his face suddenly alert and hard, his mouth set and stern.

Tony's colleagues were delighted to have a pretty woman with whom to discuss the business in hand, but they were set in their ways and regarded anything progressive as something suspicious.

'You've been a great help, Rachelle,' Tony told her when he was driving her home much later. 'You managed to convince them that the whole scheme has to be artistic as well as practical. I hope your husband didn't mind us borrowing you for the evening. Incidentally, may I say how lucky he is?'

Rachelle hesitated, then said carefully, 'Pete might not be as enthusiastic as I am about carrying on with my profession, but his work is all-demanding and I feel I want something to make a go of, if you know what I mean? Besides which, you'll need someone experienced in your beauty salon.'

He agreed, with an admiring glance at her delicate features.

'Decorative too,' he added with some satisfaction.

Rachelle made her way to the flat knowing that the job she sought was hers, yet somehow there was no elation. A peep into the lounge told her that Grandpa had gone to bed, but Pete was still up. He had fallen asleep while reading a book on the settee. One arm rested along the back, showing a nice smooth masculine brown hand with well-shaped long fingers that could caress or show amazing strength in its grip.

She looked longingly at the dark hair, rough and tousled, his eyelids fringed with thick black lashes presenting a different picture, a more boyish one, than the man she knew. He could be so many things—arrogant, hard, tender, loyal, generous and proud. Rachelle sighed.

Despite his height, width of shoulder and superior strength, Rachelle wanted to take him in her arms protectively. Her heart was doing all manner of silly antics and a wave of tenderness swept over her as exquisite and painful as a sword thrust. In that moment she would have grovelled in the dirt and oil which she hated, anything to be with him. She hovered over him with bated breath, then suddenly the spell was broken. Pete stirred and opened his eyes.

Rachelle, taken aback with burning cheeks, retreated palpitatingly. Between those black lashes his grey eyes were tempered steel as he looked her insolently up and down.

'Well, well,' he drawled. 'So you do come home sometimes. Come and sit down and tell me all about it.'

Rachelle had not drawn back far enough to be out of his reach. The long arm draped along the settee came to life and her wrist was gripped mercilessly. Relentlessly he drew her towards him and pulled her down beside him.

She looked at him resentfully and rubbed her wrist free from the imprint of his fingers.

'It was a business appointment,' she snapped, immediately on the defensive. 'I had dinner with Tony Spelling and his co-directors.'

His eyes narrowed. 'Taking you into partnership, is he?'

'Of course not! I went with him to see the buildings at the art centre and he asked me out for dinner this evening.'

'Wants you to earn your appointment, does he?'

Rachelle's face blushed delicately. 'That's a rotten

thing to say, and you've no right to say it!'

'Haven't I? I have, you know. I've the right to do this too.'

Before she realised what was happening he had her across his knees, firmly pinned down with her legs along the rest of the settee. He began by kissing the hollow of her throat after tearing off the flimsy wrap. Then his head blotted everything out and he claimed her mouth.

At the first touch of his lips she had stiffened in an effort to hold out against him, but the old magic of his nearness was too much allied with his clean masculine fragrance. Her heart was threatening to beat a hole in her ribs and she stood out against him as long as she could. When she ceased resisting his hand moved to her back, his kisses became gentle as they deepened.

When he finally released her she had no breath for words and could only stare up at his dark, sardonic face with all the old helplessness to which his kisses always reduced her.

'I think that's wiped his kisses away,' said Pete quietly after a few moments of palpitating silence.

'Tony didn't kiss me,' she managed at last. 'I've had enough of men.'

'Have you? Shall we prove you wrong?'

He bent his head again and she struggled, taking advantage of his slackened hold. He let her free and laughed, and in the bemused state which this encounter had evoked Rachelle was lifted high on a wave of anger.

'You've gone too far!' she gasped, raising an unsteady hand to her ruffled hair.

His well cut mouth narrowed into a thin hard line. 'I would have said I haven't gone far enough.' His eyes were hard. 'Don't tempt me.'

'It wouldn't do you any good,' she retorted. 'I'm determined to live my own life.'

'You're my wife and I keep what is mine,' he reminded her forcibly. 'That fact that your mercenary little soul requires more money and the comforts involved is irrelevant. I know it must be a big temptation when you meet someone like Tony Spelling, but there's no go.'

Rachelle struggled to her feet, shaking with anger. 'Don't you dare interfere with my life! I'll ... I'll do something desperate if you do!'

He looked up at her lazily. 'Like what? Going off with Tony Spelling?' He shook his head, his smile awry. 'I'm afraid he's too much involved in making more money to get into trouble with one of his lady loves.'

She stamped her foot. 'I'm not one of his lady loves! I don't know what kind of a game you're playing, but it won't get you far, not with me. I'm going to bed.'

In her room Rachelle suddenly felt deflated. Too much had happened in one day, the most important thing being Tony Spelling practically promising her a job. She ought to be going singing to bed instead of feeling thoroughly fed up with everything. Slipping off her shoes, she lay back on the bed. The strain of the day began to tell on her and her eyes closed. She told herself that Pete was selfish, like all men. He had taken Grandpa out for the day and ignored her presence completely, yet he was angry with her for going out that evening on her own. Men! she thought disgustedly, and went to sleep.

A good night's rest seemed to benefit everyone but

Rachelle. Her grandfather was looking better and admitted to enjoying a good night. This cheered her up and she went out of her way to be pleasant to Pete. Outwardly she was the loving and contented wife with Pete playing up to her with tongue in cheek and, at times, an infuriating lift of those dark brows at her endearments.

Breakfast over, Pete told Rachelle to leave the dishes for Mrs Carne and get ready to go out. He was taking them to the races. The day was warm and sunny ideal for a day out and, for her grandfather's sake, Rachelle was determined to make the day a successful one.

To her surprise and relief her mother arrived just before they were ready to leave. Pete had apparently invited her to spend the day with them. Minnie was delighted. She adored a small flutter on the racecourse.

'I've missed you, Dad,' she said to Sam, who was looking well in his grey suit.

Minnie, perfectly turned out in shell pink, looked small, frail and slender against the tall dignified figure of her father. Rachelle hid a smile when her mother latched on to the tall loose-limbed Pete and left her to partner her grandfather.

The day was a very successful one for them all. Their small bets on the horses, along with Pete's bigger one, came up and there was champagne all round.

They all went out to dinner that evening. There was a cabaret and dancing. Minnie took Pete off to partner her for most of the evening. Pete had to lower his head some distance to talk to her, but the two of them were in conversation for most of the time that they danced.

Rachelle, content to sit with her grandfather, wondered what they were discussing so earnestly, and hoped it was her grandfather. It distressed her greatly to think of him going back into a home. An awkward moment came when Pete asked her to dance. The last thing she wanted was to be held in his arms, but with Sam enjoying his cheroot and beaming on them benignly, she had no other option than to consent.

They danced in silence, neither of them being inclined to talk. It was sufficient for Rachelle to be held in Pete's arms, but the strain of remaining aloof was great. With her grandfather present there was need for pretence, but he was not there, so it did not matter. Maybe that was what Pete was thinking too. But Rachelle did not care. The time was all too short as he drew her against him protectively when other couples came too close.

Minnie came to the flat for coffee and Pete drove her home. When he returned Sam had gone to bed and Rachelle was in the kitchen washing up the cups and saucers. He lit a cigarette in the lounge as he waited for her to return. She did so reluctantly, staring at the back of his well-shaped head as he stood going through the records by the record player. It was left to Rachelle to speak.

'Thanks for a nice day,' she said coolly. 'I think we all enjoyed it, especially Grandpa.'

There was a short silence while Pete turned round and blew a line of cigarette smoke towards the ceiling. His eyes narrowed across the room as she stood hesitatingly in the doorway.

His mouth thinned. 'For heaven's sake come in the room,' he growled. 'I don't bite. I don't know what's the matter with you. You wanted your independence, which you have to a certain extent, and the job you want is in the offing. Yet you aren't happy. How come?'

Rachelle felt his mockery and wished he would not select her out for different treatment from that he used for anyone else. Pete in this particular mood tried her fortitude to the limit. Furthermore, being with him in the warm intimacy of the flat gave her bitter-sweet reminders of the life they had led together and would still have had if things had turned out differently.

'I'm not aware of being any different from what I've always been,' she answered huskily.

'No,' he jeered. 'We always carried on our conversations with each other with one of us standing in the doorway.' He bent to stub out his cigarette in an ashtray nearby with more force than was necessary, then added, 'Come here. I want to talk to you.'

Rachelle felt her inside churn over sickeningly; she was right in the middle of a situation she had wanted to avoid; ever since coming to the flat she had dreaded such a confrontation which she was not ready for. Her eyes were wide and anguished as their eyes met and his drew her across the room.

'I'm ... tired, so make it short,' she said weakly.

Pete strode across the room to meet her and placed his hands upon her shoulders.

'Damn it, Rachelle,' he said quietly, 'I'm not an ogre. I ...'

He broke off as Sam staggered in. His face was grey.

'Sorry,' he mumbled, 'but I think I'll have to go to hospital.'

He tried to make it to the settee and would have fallen had it not been for quick action on Pete's part. He was across the room in a trice and helping Sam on to the settee, and quick as a shot Rachelle was pouring out a brandy to give to her grandfather. A wave of remorse swept over her for not being more aware that he had seemed increasingly troubled of late. He had not looked at all well at times.

To add to her distress Pete waved the brandy aside.

'Fetch some water,' he said, taking pills from the small packet in the pocket of Sam's dressing gown.

Ten minutes later they were on their way to the hospital with Rachelle sitting beside her grandfather wishing she could help in some way and knowing that she could not. She felt more unhappy than she had ever felt in her whole life before. But Pete had charge of the situation. When they arrived at the hospital Sam was admitted with the minimum of waiting, thanks to Pete, who knew who to contact to get things moving. Sam was put in a private ward and they sat down to wait.

Rachelle whispered, 'Ought we to let Mother know?'

Pete shook his head. 'We'll wait a while. This has been coming on for some time now.'

Rachelle eyed him indignantly. 'You mean Grandpa has been ill and you didn't tell me?'

'That's right,' laconically.

She bit hard on her up and turned slowly to face him, and for a long moment she met the steel in his serious grey eyes.

'But why?' There were tears in her eyes and his voice softened.

'Sam didn't want to worry you,' he said gently.

'But Mother and I had a right to know. How ill is he?'

'I don't know.' Pete slipped an arm about her shoulders. 'He's had tests and they were waiting for something to happen before they admitted him to the hospital.'

'Well, that's something,' said Rachelle in a voice which was not quite steady. 'I only hope ...'

Her voice trailed away and they sat in silence. She began to feel restless because she wanted reassurance about her grandfather's illness. It was impossible to feel cool in the overheated room—or was it because Pete's arm around her was making normal breathing difficult? She felt the palms of her hands suddenly sticky in the cold sweat of fear.

It was a long time later when they were told that Sam was going to be all right. He was to stay in hospital for a few days, then they could have him home. They arrived back at the flat in the small hours and Rachelle went to her room with the feeling that it had all been a dreadful dream.

She realised that Pete had not invited her grandfather to stay at the flat to embarrass her or force her back into his arms. He had brought him to be near to the hospital. That first day they had gone out together they had spent at the hospital while Sam had tests to discover the nature of his illness.

There had been the pills too that Pete had brought for Sam on his first morning at the flat. But everything was going to be fine now that Grandpa was going to be all right again. Nothing else mattered, not even the fact that her own heart was nearly breaking if she stopped to think about it.

Rachelle had crawled into bed to stare with aching eyes into the gloom. A sob rose in her throat, and she choked it back with difficulty. A few days ago she had had such high hopes of beginning a career again; Tony Spelling's promise of a job had lifted her on the crest of a wave. But she had not reckoned on her love for Pete getting in the way. Riding on the crest of a wave had been shortlived. It had curled over to fling her on to the hard ground of reality.

Those castles in the air from which she was to look back on the grime and struggle with Pete were no more. Sitting there at the hospital with Pete's arm around her, his deep voice vibrating against her, had decided her that she wanted his love more than anything else in the world. She wished now that she had kept closer to Sam, asked his advice.

Sleep was still miles away when Pete came in, wearing his robe and bearing a warm drink. She blinked as he switched on the light, and sat up to pull the sheet over her bare shoulders.

'I've brought you a drink to help you to sleep,' said Pete. 'Sam is going to be all right.'

He sat on the edge of the bed and put the drink into her hand.

'Thanks,' she said on a dry throat. 'I ... I ...'

Her hand began to tremble and the tears poured down her face.

'Hey now!' he said gently as he rescued the cup. 'Come on, drink it down. If it's bothering you about me sleeping here forget it. I'm using Sam's room.'

But Rachelle was sobbing, close to hysteria. Her teeth rattled against the edge of the cup and after one gulp she pushed it away.

'I can't seem to keep ... from ... from trembling,' she stammered.

Pete put the cup down. 'Delayed shock,' he told her. 'It happens. You must think an awful lot of your grandfather.'

The next moment he had shed his robe and was in

bed beside her, gathering her into his arms. Rachelle closed her eyes with the feeling that she had come home, and slept.

CHAPTER FOUR

RACHELLE opened her eyes, felt them feeling odd, then she recalled her weeping the previous night. Slowly her head turned and she saw the dent on the edge of the pillow beside her own where Pete had rested while holding her in his arms.

She quivered as she remembered his gentle hold as he had comforted her as he would have done a child. He had told her days ago that he did not want what she would not give freely. Had he meant that, or was it just an excuse for his cool behaviour towards her? He had called her mercenary because she was sensitive to dirt and noise.

Rachelle had never visualised the kind of man she would fall in love with, and in retrospect it was difficult to say at exactly what moment this wonderful but frightening thing had happened. True, at their first meeting she had felt the stirring of something strange happening to her, a kind of breathlessness and pride that he had somehow chosen her for the evening.

The first time he had taken her out she had told him about her father dying two years before, about Grandfather who had lost his wife and lived at home with her mother and herself, and her own ambition to own her own beauty parlour once she had qualified.

Maybe if Pete had met her wearing oil-stained slacks

and shirt she would have decided that beauty culture and oil rigs did not exactly mix. But he had sat opposite to her at the immaculate candlelit table in one of the high-class restaurants in the West End of London with the handsome, well-groomed look which undoubtedly added ten per cent to the bill.

Not that Rachelle was really mercenary. Training for a job she knew she would love was a stepping stone for something worthwhile in life. Then Pete had taken her to a theatre and supper, after which they had walked back to her home. At her door he had taken her into his arms and she had gone up to her room treading on pink clouds. He had proposed and she was to marry him immediately. Just like that.

In the clear cold light of day romance belonged to candlelit restaurants and moonlit nights. Rachelle had taken fright, resenting a trip into the unknown to an unexplored foreign land with someone who was practically a stranger. But the next time they had met she had known that she was sunk. It was already too late to back out. She washed and dressed, thinking about her grandfather. Pete had said he was going to be fine, so on this confident note she walked into the kitchen.

Breakfast was ready and Pete was scanning a newspaper. He looked up as she came to the table and put down the paper.

'Help yourself to whatever you want,' he said pleasantly but with no warmth. 'We're going to pay Minnie a visit to tell her about her father. I don't suppose she'll want to go to the hospital, since she hates them, but she might want to come here until Sam comes out.'

Rachelle lowered herself into her chair and bit her lip. Pete was as cold as the snows. Had she expected him to be anything else after letting him believe the previous evening that her tears and emotional state were all for her grandfather?

She sipped her fruit juice and nearly choked on it, and watched him pick up a letter by his plate. He perused the closely written pages swiftly, then returned the pages to the envelope without comment.

Because she knew that toast would stick in her throat, Rachelle took a fried egg and a slice of beautifully cooked ham and did her best to eat it. She managed the egg and part of the ham before turning to her coffee. Beyond telling her to leave the explanation of Sam's illness to him when they went to fetch her mother, Pete maintained an air of silence. They were in the car on their way to collect Minnie when Pete said coolly, 'I have to go back to my job soon. When Sam is well enough to come home I shall be leaving.'

Rachelle had carefully built up a lightheartedness she was far from supporting during the journey, telling herself that when Grandpa was about again there was no reason why she should not carry on with her plans and find a flat of her own. But with Pete gone out of her life her future happiness became of the eggshell quality, vulnerable and uncertain, easily broken.

The misery eating her inside was something she would never rid herself of if she were to flood it out with tears for the rest of her life. As for Pete, he was an unknown quantity, keeping his thoughts to himself with the strength of a man who knew where he was going.

Minnie was still in bed when they arrived and Rachelle let them in with her key. She was cross at first on being woken up. Slowly she opened her eyes with a smothered protest, looking very attractive in a filmy nightie.

'Trust you to steal in and frighten the life out of me!' she gasped malevolently. 'What time is it, and why didn't you telephone?'

'It's eleven o'clock. Time you were up,' Rachelle said.

Minnie's eyes widened as she pushed herself up in bed.

'Did you bring Pete with you?' she demanded, and when Rachelle nodded, she added, 'I suppose you've decided to come together again and make up your differences. About time too! You don't know when you're lucky, my girl, though why you have to wake me up at this unearthly hour, I can't even guess. Fancy coming and taking me by surprise like this! I simply can't see Pete until I'm respectable. I . . .'

'Mother,' Rachelle cut in patiently, 'it is now midmorning and Pete is probably in the kitchen getting your breakfast. I wouldn't say any more if I were you until you hear why we've come.'

Minnie paused in the act of getting out of bed and reaching for her wrap. She was wide awake now.

Grimly she said, 'So you haven't made it up. You're going to get a divorce? I knew it! You've had that divorced look on your face ever since you arrived.'

Rachelle laughed. 'Mother, please, stop upsetting yourself! It's nothing like that.'

Unconvinced, Minnie padded to the bathroom, had a quick wash and put on an attractive housecoat. Running a comb through her hair, she then hastily applied the minimum of make-up.

'There, I suppose that will have to do. Where's Pete?'

By the time she had eaten her breakfast while Pete and Rachelle had coffee, Minnie was fairly resigned to hear the worst. She was indignant at first at not being told about Sam, but Pete had her smiling and forgiving in no time.

'So that was why Dad rushed off to the old folks' home—because he felt ill and didn't want to give me the bother?' She sighed. 'I still feel awful about it, though.'

'And so you should,' Pete put in calmly, and lit a cheroot. 'Your remark about selling the house and taking a flat had a profound effect upon him. He had an emotional blockage in his throat and acute indigestion. There's nothing radically wrong with him at all physically.'

Rachelle gasped with indignation. 'Why didn't you say so instead of letting me torture myself that Grandpa was going to die?'

Pete said coolly, 'We're all going to die eventually. I did tell you there was nothing to worry about concerning Sam, but even I won't be sure until we have the final word from the hospital.'

Rachelle had turned to face Pete, a challenge in her eyes. The morning sun brought a halo around her hair, turning it into the colour of autumn leaves. Her blue eyes were dark pools of anger. Suddenly it was all too much. A sulden wave of misery engulfed her, and to her own surprise she burst into tears.

Minnie said hastily, 'Come with me while I dress. I'm going back with you to the hospital. If what you say is true, Pete, it's up to me to do something about it. Poor Dad!'

The telephone rang at that moment and Pete went to answer it. The call was for him, long-distance.

Minnie steered her daughter determinedly to her bedroom. While Rachelle sniffed despondently and mopped her eyes, she rummaged in the wardrobe for a dress.

'I don't know what you're crying about,' she said briskly. 'I'm the one who ought to cry for being so stupid.'

'You aren't the only one who's stupid.' Rachelle swallowed on an aching throat. 'It must run in the family.'

She hesitated, longing to confide in someone, but decided that this was one of those things she could not discuss with her mother. Minnie, emotionally involved at the moment with her father, would not be as receptive or sympathetic as one would wish.

She said dismally, 'I do hope Grandpa is all right as Pete seems to think. I have a feeling that my husband will be taking Grandpa back with him when he leaves, providing he's well enough to travel.'

Minnie slipped into a model dress in pearl grey and turned for Rachelle to zip her up at the back.

'Observant, aren't you?' Minnie commented, smoothing the dress down over her hips and eyeing herself in the long mirror. 'No wonder you're despondent. I think Dad must be too. He could be behaving like this to get his own way.'

'That's nonsense,' cried Rachelle indignantly. 'It's also a despicable thing to say about your own father when you know what a dear he is. The trouble is you can't see what's under your nose!'

Minnie trod into absurd high-heeled sandals. 'You can't see what's under your nose either,' she snapped. 'Pete adores you and you can't see it.'

'Oh, Mother!' Rachelle cried in despair. 'You only see what you want to see. Pete doesn't love me. He loves his job. It's his whole life.' There was a sudden and unexpected break in her voice. 'I ought to know— I've lived with him.'

She moved to peer into the mirror her mother had

been using and made up her ravaged face marred by tears.

'He ought to have married someone like Nancy Bigland,' she continued.

Minnie picked up her handbag. 'And who is Nancy Bigland?' she asked curiously.

'A sexpot who's mad on oil drilling—kind of freakish really—big hips, big breasts, a tiny waist that would put Marilyn Monroe to shame along with her wiggle. Her father, Jesse Bigland, revelled in wildcat oilstrikes. He died six months ago. He was Pete's partner. Now Nancy is.'

Unsympathetically, Minnie murmured, 'Sounds an ideal match to me. Then you haven't a thing to worry about. You can go on with your career as you've planned.' She smiled brightly. 'If you're ready ...?'

Rachelle never knew how she got through the rest of the week. Pete had been right about her grandfather. There was nothing physically wrong with him. Minnie had been truly repentant about her part in his going away and now insisted upon him going back home. They were eating out to celebrate.

Pete leaned forward across the dining table to light a cheroot for Sam. 'Why not let him stay in the flat I have on lease? I have it for as long as I want and he'll have the excellent Mrs Carne to look after him. Later I'm hoping he'll come over to stay with us and also pay a visit to my folks in Calgary. You'd like that, wouldn't you, Sam?'

Minnie said curiously, 'You never mention your family, Pete. I believe you didn't take Rachelle to meet them either.'

'That's right.' Pete lighted his own cheroot and tossed Minnie a narrow-eyed look. 'My folks are ranchers, but I preferred oil. My old man took umbrage and we quarrelled. However, I might be giving up the prospecting and going back to ranching.'

Rachelle turned surprised blue eyes to collide with his cool grey ones. He had spoken of her grandfather visiting them as if she was going back with him, but it was news to hear that he was thinking of packing it all in. Maybe it was just another ploy on his part to give her an excuse to break with him and to go their separate ways. Knowing Pete and his pride Rachelle just could not see him going back home admitting to failure both in prospecting and marriage.

There would have to be a good reason for his change of mind.

A woman? Nancy Bigland? It was possible. Pete adored children, and Nancy had the figure, big-boned, broad hips, for bearing him a brood of sons. Rachelle felt sick when she recalled her own miscarriage.

Sam was saying, 'I'd like to stay on in your flat, Pete, for at least a week since I have to go to the hospital for a last check-up then. As you say, Mrs Carne will be fine and it will give Minnie a rest.'

His look towards his daughter was without rancour, but her face went scarlet. 'You were never any trouble, Dad, you know that. You were so helpful around the house.'

Rachelle said tenderly, 'That's right, Grandpa. She has no one to zip her up when you aren't there!'

Aware of Pete's steely gaze, Rachelle lowered her eyes. The restaurant with its floor show and dancing was exclusive, the orchestra dreamy.

Pete smiled and took her arm. 'What about a dance before we leave?' He was still smiling when he had led her out on to the dance floor and placed an arm around her. 'I'm glad you sided with Minnie over making it up to Sam. He needs to feel wanted.'

Rachelle nearly retaliated by saying, Don't we all? Instead she found herself again siding with Minnie.

'Mother means well and ... she was trying to ... well, it doesn't matter, does it, now Grandpa is out of that dreadful home?'

His arm tightened around her. 'Sam is a very lucky man to have your love. You do have the capacity for true love, my sweet. Pity it doesn't run to a husband.'

'I don't know what you're talking about,' she answered, not looking up at him.

'Let's put it this way. If you dislike my work you don't have to dislike me.'

She lifted blue eyes to meet his in surprise. 'I don't dislike you. Why should I? We ... we have no claim on each other.'

'But you have ... I have. Doesn't that make any difference?'

Rachelle lowered her eyes to hide her confusion, and said calmly, 'I have no right to dislike your work or to dislike you for not falling in with my plans. After all, it's in the past. What we have to do now is concern ourselves about the future.'

Pete brought his lips down to her hair and laughed softly.

'I don't know whether to kiss you or beat you. You really are an unpredictable creature!'

'So are you,' she retorted. 'I didn't know about you planning to quit your job in favour of ranching. Not that it's anything to do with me. What you do or have done is your own affair.'

'Wouldn't you like to make it your affair, my sweet?' he whispered.

He was goading her on, she knew, taking the mickey out of her for running out on him. He would never forgive her that.

She said wearily, 'We don't have to go all through it again, do we? You were right when you said your world wasn't my kind; so I can't be sure yet what is my kind of world. I have to find out. I might be chasing in the wrong direction, using my job as a stopgap until I go home again to Mother. And there's just a possibility that you might change your work in my favour and then regret it.'

He said curtly, 'Who said I was changing my job for you? You left me, my sweet; it's up to you to come back. If your love for me is so weak that it quails before a struggle to make good then I don't want it.'

He left the next morning and they all went to see him off at the airport. Rachelle went for her grandfather's sake. He looked so happy and contented that she had not the heart to wipe the smile from his face by refusing to go.

Pete's bags were weighed in and they all had coffee in the airport lounge. Then his flight was called as he had to go through to Customs. and he picked up a briefcase. Minnie kissed him, Sam shook hands warmly and was touched to see him go. Then it was Rachelle's turn. Minnie and her father moved away and Pete's face, no longer wearing the charming smile put on for their benefit, changed to a smirk of irony.

'The last rites,' he whispered, and hauled her close in a grip which bruised. The cruel impact of his kiss shocked her into stillness.

His leavetaking left her numb for days. His embrace, given with leashed violence, was something that remained with her. Sam was happy at the flat with Mrs

Carne to see to his needs. He had discovered to his delight that she played chess so she became a stand-in for
his neighbour at home.

Feeling depressed, Rachelle went in search of a flat.
and it did nothing to boost her morale when she saw
the impossible prices of suitable places. She met Tony
Spelling on the third day and told him about her mis-
sion over lunch. He soon comforted her on that score
by promising her one of the luxury flats over the new
art centre.

So Rachelle was now faced with a waiting period
until the whole project was completed. Apart from the
company of her grandfather there was nothing to take
her thoughts from Pete. It was shattering how she
missed him. Never had she felt so bereft, wallowing in
a kind of misery in which she positively ached for him.

She could see him so clearly, the dark springy rich-
ness of his hair, his eyes tender, mocking, or filled with
devilment, his mouth humorous or stern, his strong
hands, the muscles rippling beneath a skin of bronze
satin, his firm brown throat that her lips had caressed
in an ecstasy of tenderness. How could she ever forget
the feel of him, his hands caressing her, his arms holding her soft yielding body against his hard one, his
mouth on hers?

A week went by during which Rachelle came to
terms with her parting from Pete. It left her with
doubts about whether she had the capacity for loving
or being happy. She had been restless and unhappy
with him in his own environment, had longed to
escape and had gone. Yet now she was on the brink of
a new life she was teetering on the brink, with that
awful restlessness more apparent. Was she deluding
herself by hoping to stem that restlessness in a new
job?

Her grandfather had been pronounced fit at the hospital; his illness had been psychological. Rachelle was both relieved and happy and kept him happy by taking him out each day. It had been easy to convince him that her parting from Pete was only a temporary one, but it had not been so easy to stop herself from turning round in a crowd of pedestrians when a deep voice remarkably like his had hit her ears like a gong.

Thanks to her grandfather her days were filled. It was the long nights which gave her nightmares, as she lay wondering if Pete was sharing his bed with someone else. Minnie came for the weekend on Saturday. After dinner in the evening Sam played a game of chess with Mrs Carne, who had been well trained in the game by her late husband. Minnie left them in the lounge and followed Rachelle into her bedroom. She had sensed her daughter's unhappiness all through dinner, but said nothing.

With a bright smile she imparted her news. 'I've had a letter from Geoff,' she announced. 'Where do you think he is?'

Listlessly Rachelle sat down on the bed to manicure her nails. 'Where is he now—up a gum tree?'

Her brother had worked his way around the world after giving up a steady job in a bank, and now he was twenty-five Rachelle thought it was time he settled down. He had done most things from lumberjacking to dish-washing, and his wanderings had been helped by an indulgent mother.

Minnie laughed and picked up a crystal scent spray from the dressing table to use it. She sniffed.

'This smells exclusive. I will say this for you, you've kept yourself sophisticated and nice.'

'Thanks. What's the latest on my dear brother?' Rachelle asked.

Minnie said airily—too airily, 'Oh, didn't I tell you? He's in Calgary.'

Rachelle's blue eyes widened. 'You ... you mean ...?'

Minnie nodded and put down the scent spray. 'At the moment he's staying with Pete's family on their ranch. Then he's going to drive over to see Pete. According to what he says it's a hundred or so miles from Calgary.'

Rachelle went a trifle pale as Minnie went to sit by her on the bed.

'Apparently Geoff has no idea that you and Pete have parted. He has learned the art of wood carving during his travels and has whittled the Lone Ranger on his horse which he intends shall be for your first-born son.'

Rachelle's blue eyes hardened. 'Just like him, isn't it? He's out of touch for years, then he calmly comes back like a doting uncle to the ... the son ... I haven't got.'

Rachelle's last few words were muffled in the hands covering her face, and Minnie drew her head against her.

'There, there,' she said softly, 'don't distress yourself. I know how you felt when you lost the baby, but it was for the best, since you and Pete are parted.' She laid her cheek on the silky hair, and went on, 'I suppose it's no use asking you to come with me to visit Pete and see Geoff? I'd like to see him. He doesn't appear to be coming home yet and while your grandpa is happy with Mrs Carne it's a good opportunity to go over there.'

Rachelle lifted tear-drenched eyes and wiped them childishly with the tip of her finger.

She said huskily, 'If you're thinking that Pete will tell Geoff that we've separated, you're wrong. Pete never talks to anyone about his private life.' She gave a sad smile. 'He'll probably accept the gift from Geoff and promise to keep it for his son.'

'And you won't come with me? After all, you're at a loose end waiting to begin your new job, or don't you think it's a good idea?'

Minnie's voice trembled hopefully. There was one thing about her mother, Rachelle thought with a lifting of her spirits, she was terribly transparent. There was nothing devious about her. She might irritate and drive you to distraction with her naïve ways, but she was honest and open.

Rachelle sniffed back her tears. 'As a matter of fact I think it's a good idea, only I don't like the thought of you going all that far alone.'

Minnie sighed. 'Well, I don't want to take Dad with me at the moment. He's settling down nicely here at the flat for a while, and he's been emotionally upset.'

Rachelle nodded. 'I see what you mean. Grandpa might think you want to get rid of him and are loading him on to Pete for a while.'

Suddenly her lips curved; Minnie had forgotten how very attractive her daughter was. Her hair beneath the light had the gleam of autumn leaves, her clear skin glowed like a pearl, and her blue eyes deepened in colour as they suddenly sparkled. Obeying a spontaneous maternal urge, Minnie put an arm around the slender waist and hugged her.

'You're a lovely creature,' she said. 'I don't know what you have to be sad about. You have all the world before you. You aren't afraid of your own husband, are you, and if it's money you're worried about, I'll pay your fare.'

'I have money of my own.' Rachelle laughed, a sweet bell-like sound. 'I'll go with you. Why not?'

CHAPTER FIVE

THE journey had been uneventful until Geoff met them in the big tourer to drive them to Pete's place. Minnie had become emotional on seeing her son again, but now she was seated beside him while Rachelle took a back seat. Geoff had the same light colouring as his mother. Of medium height, he had a boyish grin which had stood him in good stead during his wanderings.

Minnie, ever proud of her son, decided that his hair was too long and his jeans were worn—too worn for a son of hers to be seen in.

Aloud she asked, 'What are Pete's parents like, and what sort of a time did you have?'

'Very nice people,' Geoff replied without taking his eyes off the road. 'There's a daughter, Betty, aged twenty-one.'

'Pretty, is she?' Minnie asked thoughtfully.

'I suppose so. She's artistic—makes costume jewellery as a hobby.'

'Sounds interesting,' put in Rachelle from the back seat. 'You two could set up an arts and craft shop between you, what with your wood carving and her jewellery.'

Minnie said hastily, 'I can't see Geoff behind a counter. He's too adventurous.' She half turned in her seat to address her daughter. 'Have you met Pete's sister? I must say it's strange that they never made any attempt to contact you.'

It was Geoff who answered. 'Pete's old man is stubborn. He's set in his ways and they didn't see eye to eye. It seems Pete left home to earn money to buy a partnership with his father, and the old man was upset about it.'

He went on talking, but Rachelle was not listening. She was gazing out at familiar country and seeing again the green field on a rise which Pete had leased for seven years for drilling with an option to renew if he found oil. There had been oil there, but there had also been water—too much water. It had not been worthwhile going into debt for expensive equipment to pump it out.

Rachelle conceded with a pang that Pete had also had a rough time. At first she had really tried to help him, even to volunteering to work in the shack serving as a kitchen on the drilling site. But Pete had drawn the line at her working to prepare mountains of food for hungry drill crews, and engaged a man.

Undaunted, she had changed from a refined delicately attired person to one in jeans and check shirts. Looking her up and down with tongue in cheek, Pete had remarked that she still looked like something from *Vogue*. But she could cook and also make a home comfortable for him when he came in dead tired from his job. The wooden bungalow, with a veranda and big picture windows framing distant hills and woods, was furnished with a modern kitchen, deep-freeze and cabinets. Deep comfortable chairs and settees in the spacious lounge room were bright with cushions matching the sheepskin rugs on the polished wooden floor.

Geoff was swinging the car off the main highway on to a rough dirt track at reduced speed. It was not long before a line of oil derricks came into view, marching across a distant field. The 'Bigland-Standring Corp. Inc.' was a company formed by Jesse Bigland when he took Pete into partnership. Now Jesse was dead, leaving his daughter Nancy as the biggest shareholder next to Pete.

They were passing the small office on the site when a broad-shouldered, overalled figure emerged to drop down the steps to the field. He paused for a moment to stare curiously at the car, pushing his hat to the back of his head as he did so. Rachelle recognised him as Jake Denver, the head driller, who had shares in the company. She raised a hand in greeting, and he returned it with a broad grin.

He was good-looking in a bold kind of way, a Bigland man. Rachelle had always felt that he did not care much for Pete and she knew the feeling was mutual. Pete was indifferent to Jake in the way that he was to anyone—to anyone who he felt was not sincere. Pete's attitude made him strong and a man to be reckoned with. It also, in her opinion, made him the most irritating and lovable creature she had ever met. There was no compromise with Pete. He weighed up all the pros and cons, made up his mind and that was that. He had probably done that about their marriage.

Geoff ran the car to a stop at the bungalow so familiar to Rachelle. He was taking the luggage from the car trunk when they were confronted by a young slender figure in the doorway who crossed the veranda hesitantly.

Geoff grinned as he hauled out the suitcases. 'Well, I must say this is a surprise! Why didn't you say you were coming? I could have brought you. Mother, Rachelle, may I present Pete's sister, Betty. Betty, my mother and sister.'

Rachelle went forward to greet the girl warmly with a kiss. 'Hi,' she said. 'Lovely to see you at last.'

Eyes remarkably like Pete's beneath a mop of unruly dark hair laughed into hers.

'Now I know why Pete wasn't anxious to bring you home to meet his folks. You're much too lovely to be let loose among the cowhands,' she gurgled. 'And your mother looks more like your elder sister.'

Minnie offered a perfumed cheek. Now that she had found her son again, Rachelle knew she would regard it as sour grapes to find his attention wandering to someone who might take him away from her. But Betty saw nothing amiss. Taking their arms affectionately, she led them up the veranda steps into the bungalow.

Rachelle entered the large airy lounge room with its homely furnishings and tried to keep herself detached from any emotion as they all sat down. The next surprise came when an elderly woman came in with heated cheeks beneath greying hair bearing a covered tray.

'Hello, Sarah. Nice to see you're still here.' Rachelle's voice wobbled a little as she saw the friendly face. 'How are you?'

'All the better for seeing you, Rachelle,' she answered, equally overcome as she rested the tray on a low table near to where they sat. She sniffed and looked worried. 'Everybody is here. It's a little confusing.'

Rachelle said gently, 'I'm sorry if we've put you out, Sarah, but that can soon be remedied if you can't cope with extra guests.'

Sarah rubbed her chin, a habitual gesture when worried.

'It's not for me to say, but ...'

'Hello.' The juicy sexy voice accompanied the voluptuous figure into the room. 'How nice to see you even if we are, shall I say, rather overcrowded in a confined space.'

Rachelle could have giggled at the expression of surprise on Minnie's face if the situation had not been so painful. Nancy Bigland was not beautiful, her complexion was poor, but there was something dynamic about her which a man might regard as animal magnetism. True, her goods were openly displayed in a low-cut dress for the occasion, and this, allied to her red hair and dark-lashed amber eyes, sent up the temperature of any room she entered.

She was smiling at their upturned faces with a suggestion of sheathed claws about her, and Rachelle, recalling Sarah's worried frown, felt she was entitled to a little bitchiness.

With her blue eyes pointedly fixed on Nancy's bosom, she said sweetly, 'I've noticed an overspill. Any suggestions?'

The amber eyes were veiled, the voice insolent. 'Since there are only three bedrooms here, two of them small, I suggest you, Rachelle, and your companion ...'

'You mean my mother,' Rachelle put in.

'Your mother, stay at my place.'

At first Rachelle was bowled clean over by the sheer cheek of the suggestion, and the injured expression on her mother's face cried out for a refusal. But Rachelle had not lived with Pete without some of his wisdom taking root, therefore having a sobering effect on her otherwise all too hasty reactions. She saw Nancy's offer, however distasteful, as a refuge from Pete's tantalising presence in his own house.

She smiled. 'Why, Nancy,' she cried, 'that's real hospitable of you!'

'But not necessary. Thanks, Nancy, but my wife will share my room. My mother-in-law can have a bedroom along with Betty, and Geoff can sleep on the veranda or in my office.'

Pete was lolling in the doorway in a city-going suit of pale beige. He was smiling with a trace of bitter humour on his dark features. The next moment his sister Betty had flung herself at him.

'Hey!' he protested, loosening her arms from round his neck, 'you're choking me!'

Betty kissed him soundly, pulling down his head to do so.

'You beast,' she cried. 'Why didn't you keep in touch?'

He made a playful feint beneath her chin with a firm brown fist. 'I'll tell you all about it some day. And now may I greet my wife?'

He went first to Minnie and had to bend very low from his height to kiss her cheek. Then he was standing in front of Rachelle. His dark grey ironic gaze was intent upon her as he pulled her slowly to her feet with an expression she was in no condition to interpret.

'Welcome home, darling,' he murmured, and kissed her. The room spun round for Rachelle. Voices receded as cups rattled and tea was served.

The message got through to her as he released her. He did not want Betty to know about their separation. She was glad to be able to sit down, for her legs were trembling beneath her. As for Pete, he was not in the least affected by their meeting. He turned to his sister to receive a cup of tea.

'Nectar from the gods,' he drawled. 'Their reward for me propitiating them by tolerating some dreadful people.'

Minnie's eyes twinkled at him over her cup. 'Present company excepted, I hope.'

'Of course,' he answered. 'I prefer the company of animals to some business people.' He laughed at Minnie. 'Present company excepted!'

He had moved to stand beside the settee on which Rachelle sat with her mother. Ever aware of his nearness, Rachelle lowered her eyes away from his profile outlined against the wall, the lean dark line of his jaw, his well-shaped black head. All combined to give her an aching longing for him. Careful, Rachelle, her head said, while her heart went soft and mushy.

When Minnie followed Betty to the kitchen for more tea, Pete dropped into the vacant seat beside her. It was then that she noticed Nancy had gone. Geoff had also left the room, presumably to take the baggage to the bedrooms.

Retreating imperceptibly, Rachelle spoke with an assumed coldness, and put down her cup.

'I need a wash. I feel dusty and sticky.'

'You don't look it. As usual you look as though you've stepped right out of a glossy magazine.'

Rachelle was quiveringly aware that Pete was sitting on her dress and imprisoning her. The mocking light in his eyes made her feel defenceless and very young.

'That's the second nice thing you've said to me since I've arrived,' she said.

'I can be nice.' He put an arm around her. 'With the impersonal kindness of a host who likes to see his guests happy.'

Rachelle did not like the way her heart was behaving beneath his hold. He was much too near for her comfort.

'There isn't any need to put on an act when your sister is out of the room,' she said primly. 'I hate deceiving her. She's nice.'

'All girls are nice until they get married,' he said sardonically.

She stiffened. 'And what does that mean?' she asked.

Pete did not answer but continued to stare at her enigmatically until she felt like screaming.

She lifted her chin militantly. 'It's rude to stare at people,' she told him scathingly.

He laughed, and it made such a difference to his dark face. Her heart was beating alarmingly fast.

'I can't help it—you're so delicious. Your eyes are deep blue pools and your skin is like porcelain.' He touched her smooth cheek gently with the back of his fingers. 'I can't make up my mind whether I'm hooked on you or merely wanting the unattainable.'

The old magic was working, the magic of his nearness, and Rachelle had to do something about it.

She blurted, 'What about Nancy?'

He drew back and lifted a brow darkly. 'What about Nancy?'

'Surely you know by now that she's your kind of girl?'

'So what?'

Rachelle knew she should not have asked such an outrageous question and she felt ashamed. But she could not have kept the words back to save her life. It was essential for her to know the truth, even if Pete was angry with her. She had to know. Her voice lingered on the air in a husky whisper.

'Do you love her?'

She stared at his face, trying to read his controlled dark expression, and failed dismally.

'What do you want me to say? That I do? You couldn't blame me if I did, could you?' The savage tones rasped her nerves, cutting into her heart like a saw. 'I'm a normal man with needs like anyone else. You left me to go to the devil had I felt inclined. Well, you don't mean that much to me any more!'

Rachelle lost some of her colour, shocked out of her senses. There was a darkening of the room for a moment, then everything lightened as Minnie and Betty appeared with more tea. Colour came slowly back into her face, staining her cheeks into a wild rose. Her lips trembled into a smile.

'No more tea for me, thanks,' she said. 'I'd like to freshen up.'

It was imperative for her to get away from Pete in that moment. Her head felt in a whirl, and she looked appealingly at her mother.

Minnie said, 'I think I would too.'

Pete rose lazily to his feet as Geoff entered the room.

'You can entertain Geoff, Betty. I'll escort the ladies to their rooms.'

He took Rachelle's arm as she moved from his side and they went along a small corridor where Pete stopped at a door and opened it.

'Your room, Minnie,' he said with a smile. 'Betty is right next door and then the bathroom's further along. Our room, Rachelle's and mine, is opposite on the other side of the corridor there. The other doors lead to linen rooms, storage cupboards and my office. Sarah will give you anything you want, and I'll be around. Her room is at the far end of the corridor.'

Rachelle walked into the familiar room with a jolt of

her heart. It did not appear to have been touched since she went away. She gazed round with a set face.

'It ... doesn't appear to ... to have been touched since I ...'

She paused, unable to go on, and turned slowly to face Pete as he closed the door and leaned back against it.

'That's right,' he said grimly. 'Just as you left it. Sarah cleans it, you haunt it.'

'I do? Don't be silly!'

'I'm not. I've been using one of the guest rooms.'

She swallowed convulsively as he strolled over to the window.

'Pete,' she said in a husky whisper, 'I'm trying hard, but you're making it awfully difficult.'

Rachelle spoke to the back of his dark head. There in the centre of the floor she disregarded travel-weariness and a cold feeling around her heart, and tried to put her disordered thoughts in order.

He replied without turning round, 'What I don't know is exactly what you're trying for.'

'I don't know. Maybe I'll find the answer here. I ... I came with Mother because she wanted to see Geoff.' She hesitated for a moment. 'Grandpa is fine, by the way. He's at the flat for the time being. Mrs Carne is looking after him. Mother didn't want him to come with us in case he thought we were putting him on you.'

Pete said quietly, 'Sam can come any time he likes, he knows that.'

But not me, Rachelle thought unhappily. Why did he not turn round instead of staring out through the window with the air of a lonely man? For a crazy moment she wanted to ask him to give her another chance and start again, but stubborn pride kept her silent. He was too unapproachable, too menacing. Had he greeted her in a more gentle way she could have confessed to him how she felt about him. But what was the use? He had already told her that she meant nothing to him any more.

Slowly Pete turned round as though sensing the tumult and unhappiness within her, then he paused within an arm's length of her. He would have recognised her fragrance anywhere. Desire flowed through him as her pale face wavered beneath his gaze. Rachelle held her breath as his arms seemed to grope towards her, then the moment passed and he thrust his hands into his pockets.

'The whole place is full of beans at your return,' he drawled, knowing the steel in his voice matched his grey eyes. 'Nancy has arranged a party for you this evening. Be ready at seven. We're all invited.'

Rachelle looked at his dark face, not angry or even surprised—just looking steadily and frankly the way she used to look at him. She cleared her throat.

'We, that is Mother and I, have been travelling for ages and I for one am tired. I'm sure Mother will be too.'

Pete said, 'There's all of two hours before we need go. You can both rest in that time and we needn't stay late.'

In the silence which followed he saw the gleam in her blue eyes change to a hopeless kind of sadness. She stood before him as slim and lissom as a young willow. The high curve of her breast, the small waist and long slim legs belonged to the girl he had loved and married. There was a cold stream of anger flowing through him that such an exquisite creature should be all top show. She was no better than Nancy, in his estimation. Granted, Nancy advertised her charms more blatantly, but she was all woman, whereas his wife was a pretty doll to be handled with clean hands in case her fripperies got soiled.

She said in a small voice, 'I'll go and tell Mother.'

His hands fisted deep into his pockets as she turned to leave the room. Stony-faced, he watched each graceful movement, finding it unbelievable that any woman as attractive as she was could be so unselfconscious of her own body and charm. Then with squared shoulders, he went to drawers and clothes closets to select his gear for the evening from the clothes he had brought earlier that day from the guest room he had vacated in favour of his mother-in-law.

Rachelle found her mother unpacking and humming a tune.

'How do you feel about going out for a party gathering this evening? Nancy Bigland has invited us all over to her place. You needn't go if you're feeling too tired.'

Rachelle had to smile. Her mother looked about as jaded as a freshly plucked lettuce. Her grey eyes widened in pleasurable anticipation and her fingers fluttered among an assortment of bottles and jars she was arraying on her dressing table.

'I take it that plunging necklines are optional,' she remarked dryly.

Rachelle giggled. 'You mustn't take Nancy seriously. Nancy spilling out of her clothes is pure Nancy. No one takes her seriously.'

'Not even Pete?'

Minnie turned around slowly to face her daughter, and gave a wicked smile.

She went on, 'I liked the way you said overspill with

your eyes ogling Nancy's cleavage.'

Rachelle's cheeks were a warm rose. 'That was bitchy of me—especially when she invited us to stay at her place.'

Minnie cluck-clucked like a mother hen. 'For a cute gal Nancy was a bit slow in not putting up Geoff and Betty instead, leaving you in your rightful place with your husband. Still, I'm glad she didn't, and it makes me feel more kindly disposed towards her.'

'Why?' demanded Rachelle bluntly.

'My dear girl, don't be more naïve than you can help! I wouldn't like to think of Geoff and Betty being together and away from my supervision. That wouldn't do at all.'

Rachelle shook her head. 'Oh, Mother! Geoff is twenty-five and ought to be settling down. You can't keep him tied to your apron strings for ever.'

'Maybe not,' replied Minnie philosophically. 'But I don't like the family he might be marrying into. With one divorce pending—yours—I don't exactly relish two in our family.'

'That's nonsense!' protested Rachelle.

'Is it? Let me tell you something, my girl. Nancy might have all her goods in the shop window, but she makes sure that the till is correct at the end of the day. It's as plain as those oil derricks out there that she aims to come between you and Pete subtly and surely. Why do you think she invited you and me to stay with her? Think that one over while you take a rest, which is what I'm going to do now.'

Pete went softly into the bedroom. He had half an hour to wash and dress, and to put on the things he had laid out earlier on the bed. He looked towards it to find that his clothes had been placed neatly over the backs of chairs, his outer clothes hanging outside the clothes closet on hangers.

The reason was Rachelle, lying on the bed fast asleep, having bathed and put on a wrap. The dressing table top was once more arrayed with her toilet things, glittering bottles, pretty boxes with her own particular scent teasing the air.

Pete's well-cut mouth thinned. He was remembering how this room, their room, had been a corner of heaven, a haven where he had been greeted by bright eyes and loving arms. He had bathed and shaved and was back in the bedroom with a towel bound around his waist when Rachelle stirred, sensing his presence in the room.

She blinked, was suddenly wide awake and was pushing herself up in bed. Her blue eyes wide with alarm, she took in his naked torso, the well-developed shoulder muscles gleaming beneath a satin-smooth skin, the powerful hirsute chest, the tousled hair, the dark grey eyes deepening with an expression that scared her.

'If you think I'm sharing this room with you,' she croaked, 'you're very much mistaken!'

His eyes were narrowed dangerously. 'And if you expected to share it with me, you're very much mistaken as well.'

He moved easily to the bed and was about to put out an arm towards the chair nearby when she cowered away from his freshly groomed fragrance. The longing to feel his strong arms around her, to be loved, to be warm and safe against him in the silence like waves washing up on the safe shore of matrimony, was agonising enough to curl her hands into fists. If she were to draw him into bed with her now the outcome would avail her nothing.

Pete was only a man, after all. He would give way to natural instincts and end up by hating her for it afterwards. His look cut her down to size.

'No need for alarm—I wouldn't touch you with a bargepole. I'm not parading my manly charms for your benefit either. If you'd left my clothes where I put them in the first place I wouldn't have to make a tour of the room to pick them up.'

'You ... you aren't ... going to put them on in here?' she gasped.

'Why not? You've seen me undressed often enough.'

He dressed leisurely, so leisurely that she felt like yelling at him to hurry up. She heard the jingle of his car keys as he transferred his bits and pieces from one jacket to another, and after what seemed a long, long time, he was brushing his hair at the dressing table mirror.

'You'd better get dressed,' he advised. 'Time is running out to put on your pretties.'

But Rachelle stubbornly remained in bed until it began to dawn upon her gradually that it was no good playing for time. Pete in his present mood was quite capable of taking her to the party in her wrap.

Reluctantly she slid from the bed and went to get her evening dress. Then she flitted to the bathroom to put it on. The zip would stick, of course. It occurred to her that she could go along to her mother's room for help, but the thought of meeting someone on the way and looking foolish when it was known that Pete was with her stopped her in her tracks.

She returned to their room as Pete was putting on his jacket.

In a small voice she said, 'Do you mind zipping me up?'

She presented him with a beautiful back view of flimsy underwear, hardly any protection but so endearingly Rachelle. His fingers came into contact with the slender, glowing warmth of her skin as he sought to discover the cause of the zip not working. Within seconds he was sliding it upwards with ease.

Rachelle held her breath at his nearness, felt his warm breath on her hair and waited for him to lower his lips. Instead he straightened, said laconically, 'Nice dress.'

'Glad you approve.'

His hands fell from her back and Rachelle reacted to his drawing away with closed eyes. Going to the mirror to make up her face, she spoke at random.

'I thought Nancy would have been married by now. I always thought Jake Denver was sweet on her.'

Pete snapped on his wristwatch and spoke without lifting his head.

'Jake's not the marrying kind, you know that.'

Rachelle added a touch of blue above her eyes. 'Do I?'

'You also know that he's sweet on you.'

'That isn't true!' Her aim was not too good and the colouring went into her eye. She groped for a tissue and found one pushed into her hand.

Pete said raspingly, 'I don't know why you use that rubbish. Your kind of lovely eyes don't need make-up to enhance them.'

He strode from the room and came back with a water-soaked tissue. Then he lifted her chin and dabbed it on her injured eye. Rachelle sniffed as water ran down her face on to the towel he had hastily draped around her shoulders.

He held the swab there for several seconds while Rachelle tried to make up her mind whether her faint giddiness was owing to his nearness or to travel fatigue. Her heart was racing as he lifted the swab from her injured eye and raised her chin with a forefinger.

Tears trembled on the long lashes and his manner became more gentle. She looked fragile, but he knew different. He also knew that she had an appeal for him that no other woman had. Her sensitivity over life and its problems irritated him, but her enchanting sense of humour made her very desirable.

His voice was a trifle thick. 'How does it feel now?'

'Not too bad.'

'Sure?'

'Of course I'm sure.' Rachelle moved uneasily beneath his scrutiny. Her composure began to tilt.

'Your eye is bloodshot and you look pale,' he commented.

'I've had a long day ...' she began.

He released her chin, said coolly, 'You can stay home if you like.'

'Oh, for goodness' sake!' Rachelle went on with her toilet and ignored him. Her hands were not entirely steady, but when he moved away her confidence came back.

Through the mirror she caught a glimpse of his proud profile, his fine leanness, with the feeling that impassable barriers reared between them. They would be less formidable if she could be sure that Pete would meet her half way. As things were, she was pushing him into Nancy's arms.

She said, 'I've been thinking a lot about us—you and me, I mean.'

'And what conclusion did you come to, may I ask?'

'That ... that you might have been happier with Nancy.' She dusted over the light make-up and saw her eyes were dark pools of unhappiness staring back at her in the mirror.

'But I didn't marry Nancy. I married you, and what I have not done or might have done doesn't concern you, my sweet.'

'I beg to differ. Can I ask you a question?'

'About what, my dear?'

Rachelle quivered at the insolence of his voice. His manner had completely changed and they seemed to be conversing through glass.

'About Nancy—and you?' she faltered. 'What's between you?'

'Nothing.'

'But ...'

'I said nothing. You're still my wife.'

'In name only,' she reminded him. 'Everything we had is in the past, but what you do now counts, at least it does with me. If you want Nancy ... it's all right with me.'

She waited for him to answer with a surge of passionate hope that made her breathless. When he did not speak she turned.

'Pete ...'

No answer.

She was trembling when she turned back to the mirror.

The hand on her shoulder swung her round to face the grey steel flints in his eyes. His arms closed like iron bands around her and he was forcing her mouth to the will of his own. But her lips were as cold as her heart and he let her go as roughly as he had seized her.

'That's a reminder that you're still married to me,' he said grimly. 'And to think that you were once my most treasured possession!'

They were on their way to Nancy's party in Pete's car. Minnie had seated herself in the back between Geoff and Betty, leaving Rachelle to sit beside Pete. She could not look at him. The feeling of helplessness was frightening. It was like being swept along by a relentless tide of events which, without any wish of her own, bore her along with neither the power nor the will to resist.

Fortunately it was only a short journey to Nancy's place, a bungalow on a much grander scale than Pete's. Nancy was there at the door to welcome them. She looked eye-catching in a red satin dress, tight and all-revealing.

'Come on in,' she smiled. 'We're all here.'

Someone took their wraps and they joined the gathering in the spacious room. Rachelle knew most of the guests. She saw Jake Denver with the rest of the field drillers along with a field crew from a nearby field. Jake lifted a hand in greeting across the room and gave her a warm smile. Her mother did not approve.

'Nice-looking man, but I don't like the way he looks at you, darling,' she whispered.

'Jake is a womaniser,' Rachelle replied. 'We all expected him to marry Nancy after her father died.'

Minnie said grimly, 'All I can say is that it wouldn't be for want of her trying. That dress—really!'

Rachelle laughed. 'You'll get used to it.'

Minnie snorted in disgust. 'Never! You were right to leave here. This is no place for you.'

'Pete ...' Rachelle broke off and found a glass of champagne in her hand. Nancy was calling for everyone's attention and Pete spoke.

'I want you to meet my sister Betty, my wife's brother Geoff, and my wife—who needs no introduction.'

Everybody gathered round and cordially raised their glasses. Minnie had managed to stand in between her son and Betty and Rachelle quelled a smile. Jake Denver, at Rachelle's elbow, bent his mouth to her ear.

'Welcome back,' he whispered. 'We've missed you, Rachelle. Here to stay?'

'For the present,' she replied, and encountered Pete's grey glance defiantly over the rim of her glass. Was his hostile look for her or for Jake?

'You're wise,' Jake was speaking again in her ear. 'The two biggest shareholders in the company might merge if you leave the field clear for them. There's talk.'

Rachelle lowered her eyes into her glass. 'There always is in a tiny community. They have nothing else to do. How come you haven't annexed one of the two shareholders yourself?'

'Nancy can't see me for Pete. Anyway, the scenery will be much more interesting with you around.' He lifted his glass. 'To you.'

Rachelle looked up into his conceited smile, looking into dark eyes which had not the slightest effect on her emotions. They never had. With Jake she had always been friendly in an impersonal way, keeping conversation on an unemotional level. She had to rediscover the knack of turning a somewhat embarrassing conversation into one which ran on ordinary lines with an unaccountable friend or enemy.

She had never been sure which Jake was. He had

not the slightest interest in her personally, she was sure. He probably saw in her an opportunity to irritate Pete. It had been up to her to make any kind of a threat from Jake to either Pete or herself meaningless. She hoped it was fatigue from travelling that she now regarded him with a vague sense of unease coupled with apprehension.

Her smile, with Pete in mind, was disarming. 'You haven't changed, have you, Jake?' she teased. 'A lady-killer to the end. Why not try some of that sex appeal on the oil drills? How are they making out?'

Jake's look was guarded. He shrugged. 'Too much water about. But you never know. However ...' He paused, his glance became sharper and Rachelle noticed for the first time that those dark eyes were set a little too close together for her comfort. 'If you're ever hard up for cash I would happily take those shares off your hands.'

'Now that's very generous of you, considering that you think them worthless. I'll think about it. Excuse me while I talk to a much better proposition—Nancy.'

She moved gracefully across the room to where Nancy was holding court with Pete and several of the field crew.

'Hello, Bill,' she said to a hefty blond man who looked out of place off the drilling field. 'Nice to see you.'

He laughed. His smile was warm and friendly. 'All the better for seeing you, Rachelle. I bet Pete is over the moon to have you back.'

'Are you, Pete?' Rachelle laughed up into the dark face. The champagne had gone to her head since she had eaten little all day—at least that was the only explanation, she told herself, for her tantalising smile.

He looked down at her darkly. 'Ask me later this evening,' he answered with a glint in his eye.

The men guffawed and Nancy looked anything but amused. Her full lips pouted. 'Why don't we have a little dancing?' she suggested. 'Put on some music, Pete.'

Rachelle had no shortage of partners; Jake Denver danced with her for part of the evening. Minnie danced around with delight and Betty, Pete's sister, sat out for most of the time with Geoff. Rachelle wondered wistfully if they were serious about each other. She liked Betty and thought it was time that her brother settled down, but Minnie would be sure to be against the union. Another woman would take her son from her over her dead body!

Rachelle mulled this over while resting for a moment between partners. Jake had monopolised her all evening and now he had sailed away with Nancy in his arms. She had lost her problems in the music and rhythm of the dance, and was beginning to enjoy herself. She saw her mother go by in the arms of the stalwart Bill ... Betty with Geoff, looking engrossed in each other ... Jake with Nancy, who was laughing no doubt at one of his sly innuendoes, but Pete was missing. He had kept away from her all evening.

'Enjoying yourself, Mrs Standring?'

His deep voice startled her from her thoughts as he hovered above her with an expression she tried to analyse—searching, sardonic, quizzical—there was no way of knowing. His smile had a trace of bitter humour. For a few moments he had been watching the frank enchantment of her face, seen it change at his approach into a bleak regard.

'I think everyone is,' she answered.

'Not feeling tired?'

She managed a smile. 'Who am I to admit to tiredness when Mother is dancing like a teenager?'

'Then you aren't too tired to dance with me?'

Rachelle hesitated. She had not expected this—for him to ignore her presence for most of the evening and then to seek her out just when he felt like it.

'I was enjoying sitting this one out,' she answered.

'Then perhaps you'd like a drink? Coffee? Wine? Martini?'

'Whisky—neat whisky, please,' she said demurely.

The dark eyebrows shot up in startled surprise. 'You're joking, of course.'

'No, I'm not.'

His mouth quirked with suppressed amusement. 'Who are you trying to impress? Me?'

'No.'

He brought it, placed it in her hand and waited for her to drink. The smell as she raised it to her lips was more than enough.

'Aren't you having a drink?' she asked, lowering her glass.

Pete shook his head. 'Not for the moment. I'm driving.'

She had to try her drink, much as she detested it. She had only asked for it in sheer bravado, and he knew. He was smiling.

He said softly, 'Perhaps you would like to dance after all?'

Rachelle stiffened against his disarming approach and let him take the glass from her hand. Then she was in his arms, gliding smoothly across the floor. Anger, unhappiness, antagonism fled as the strains of the music filled the room and he drew her closer. She closed her eyes, feeling extraordinarily sleepy.

Pete said, 'Time you went home. You're tired.'

It was not long before they were all back in the car with Rachelle in her place beside Pete in the front seat. Gradually her eyes closed and she snuggled down against his shoulder.

CHAPTER SIX

THE sun streaming through the window alerted Rachelle to the lateness of the hour. She had overslept. Pushing herself up in bed, she saw that the pillow beside her still retained its pristine freshness. Geoff had slept on the veranda. Where had Pete slept?

She found Sarah in the kitchen. 'Lovely to have you back again,' Sarah said warmly. 'The place hasn't been the same without you. You haven't put on much weight.'

She eyed the slender figure, the small, firm pointed bust, the trim waist, and the tailored belt of Rachelle's slacks fitting snugly above the flatness of her tummy. She frowned and spooned coffee into the percolator.

'I must say,' she went on, 'your holiday doesn't appear to have done you much good. You look pale and undernourished. Pete has taken Geoff and Betty to the drilling field,' she added. 'They had a good breakfast. I hope you do.'

Rachelle helped herself from the freezer and settled down to sip orange juice.

'Bread rolls, honey and coffee will suit me fine, Sarah, please,' she said.

Sarah snorted her disapproval but did as she was told. Minnie had not put in an appearance when Rachelle had finished her breakfast, and a peep into her room showed her still sleeping.

'I'm going for a walk,' Rachelle told Sarah. 'Mother will probably be up when I get back.'

She had crossed the front veranda to descend the steps when there was the sound of footsteps behind her.

'Rachelle, just a minute! Where are you going?'

It was Nancy, clad in check shirt and black jeans. The top three buttons of the shirt were unfastened to show a plunging neckline.

'I'm going for a walk,' she replied.

'You aren't going after Pete, then? Do you know where he is? He isn't in his office.'

'No.' Rachelle did not want her company, but Nancy fell into step beside her and was obviously going with her despite whether she approved or not.

'It's very unusual for Pete to be out during the morning. He's usually in his office, unless . . .' Here she looked coyly at Rachelle. 'He might have gone over to take a dip in my new swimming pool. He's done some mornings.'

'I didn't know you had a swimming pool,' commented Rachelle.

'Oh yes. We have swimming parties. I thought Pete would have told you in his letters?'

'No, he hasn't.'

The tawny eyes slid her a sly look. 'Of course, you're out of touch with each other, aren't you? You surely don't expect to fool us all that you and Pete have made it up, do you?'

'It doesn't bother me what you believe. What Pete

and I do is our own affair,' Rachelle said tartly.

They were strolling towards the woods when Nancy said,

'I hope the career you're seeking is a success, because Pete doesn't want you back.'

Rachelle felt cold despite the warmth of the sun. 'Who told you I was after a career?' she demanded.

Nancy shrugged. 'Word gets around. Stepping stone, is it, for marriage with Tony Spelling?'

Rachelle stopped dead in her tracks. 'How do you know about Tony Spelling?' she gasped indignantly.

Another shrug. 'As I said, word gets around, and didn't Pete go to see Tony Spelling to do business with him?'

Rachelle's tones were icy. 'You appear to know an awful lot about my husband's affairs. Mine too, for that matter.'

Nancy laughed. 'Oh well, Pete and I are like that.' She held up a hand and crossed her fingers. 'You've come back too late.'

Rachelle stood looking scornfully at her companion. 'I see no point in continuing this walk with you, Nancy. If I choose to come home to join my husband there's really nothing you can do about it.' Her look at the quivering jealous face of Nancy was disdainful and filled with meaning. 'Pete not only works in his office at the bungalow, he also sleeps there.'

Nancy's mouth gaped open in disbelief. 'You mean to say that Pete could still be in bed? That he overslept?'

'Why not? He's only a man after all, and a very attractive one.'

'I don't believe it. Pete wouldn't take you back after what you've done.'

'What have I done? Lots of wives carve out a career for themselves. You know nothing about it. Pete would never tell anyone about what goes on between him and me.'

The tawny eyes flashed malevolently. 'Like to bet? Pete and I are two of a kind. We like roughing it, we like adventure and taking risks. He ought never to have married you—he knows that now.'

'Does he?' Rachelle felt her anger rising to blood heat. 'If I'm not his kind then I'm certain that you aren't. He likes adventure and taking risks, I'll agree, but he's never been partial to anything handed to him on a plate.'

She looked down meaningfully at Nancy's rounded bosom and generous curves which even the black jeans did not entirely play down. Nancy's hand came up like a flash to slap a stinging blow on her cheek.

'How dare you?' she cried. 'You're jealous! Any man who's been with me would have no use for you.' Nancy's teeth gritted together in her rage. Her eyes had the malicious satisfaction of seeing the red marks on the fine skin. 'You with your airs and graces! You don't want a real man. Go back to your city kind! We don't want you here.'

Rachelle was trembling with the unexpectedly vicious attack, but she looked her opponent straight in the eye.

She said quietly, 'You're a fool, Nancy, and your own worst enemy. You'll find that out when it's too late. Men never marry girls who are too free with their favours.'

With the feeling that her day had been spoiled before it had really begun, Rachelle left Nancy behind and walked at random. When presently she heard footsteps she quickened her own, fully expecting Nancy to catch up with her again. But it wasn't Nancy; it was Jake Denver.

'Hello there,' he said with obvious pleasure. 'I was just thinking about you.'

Meeting those bold appraising eyes, Rachelle decided that it was not going to be her day.

'I hope it was something nice,' she answered lightly, wishing him miles away.

'It was for me. I'm not so sure about the way you would take it.' He rubbed a clean-shaven jaw thoughtfully. 'On the other hand, I think you've been kidding us along.'

'I don't understand. What are you getting at? I don't want any more insults today, thank you. So if you'll just move out of my way I'll continue my stroll in peace.'

He raised a brow and folded his arms. 'You haven't met Nancy by any chance, have you?'

'Don't tell me you're after her so early in the morning?'

He grinned. 'So you did meet Nancy. She's on the warpath. She was queen of the drilling fields until you came back, and now you've pushed her nose out of joint just like you did before.'

Rachelle said icily, 'It was quite unintentional, I can assure you. Hadn't you better get back to your job?'

'You know, you do look like a queen.' His dark eyes were on her, making her feel defenceless and very naïve. 'You have the look of being above all earthly things.'

She smiled. 'If that's meant to soften me into selling you my shares in the company, you're doing very well.'

He gave a mock bow and swept one arm cavalier fashion across his chest.

'Thank you, madame,' he answered.

'Not at all,' she replied coolly. 'And now, I must be on my way—but not before telling you something I should have done long ago. I'm not very romantic where men are concerned.'

The colour rushed beneath her clear skin as she spoke the lie. It hung heavily upon her as she recalled how much she loved Pete, and how perfectly they had been matched physically. There would never be any-one else who would give her fulfilment.

Jake's eyes narrowed. 'Those red marks on your cheek?' he queried. 'What happened?'

Rachelle lifted a hand to her face. 'Nothing. Now, I must be going.'

He made no move to stop her. She had not expected him to. He knew how far he could go before having Pete to deal with. She ought never to have come back. Pete did not want her and she was only causing trouble albeit inadvertently.

A wave of depression washed over her which lasted until her return to the bungalow. On her way she passed the creek where she used to bathe and she stood for pensive moments looking down into the sparkling water. Useless to tell herself that it was only a phase that she was passing through, that when she was back home resuming her career things would sort them-selves out. Meanwhile, while Pete's sister Betty was there she had to play along with him that their marriage was happy. Pete would hate his family to know that he was an abandoned husband.

She could make her stay a short one even to persuad-ing her mother to go along with Betty to be introduced

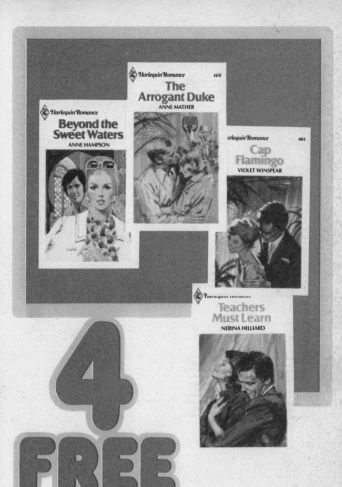

4 FREE

Harlequin Romances

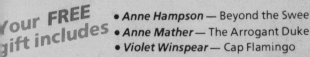

Take these  4 best-selling Harlequin Romance stories

 FREE

... EXCITING DETAILS INSIDE

to Pete's family. Then she could make some excuse like going back to see how Grandpa was going on. It would be a part truth, since her grandfather meant a lot to her.

Pete was waiting for her on the veranda looking vital and strong in his healthy tan. The bush shirt open at the firm throat was something she had to lower her gaze from since it reminded her of the times she had kissed it. She wondered if similar thoughts ran through his head each time he saw her. Ridiculous to fool herself into believing that Pete had any thoughts about her, romantic or otherwise.

He had seen her long before she had seen him from his careless posture against the veranda post. She had looked kind of lonely and forlorn. She was not the kind of sophisticated career woman she was trying to convince herself that she was. If he made her feel miserable and uncomfortable it was her own fault. There had been times when she had been in his thoughts, and if he admitted it honestly he would have to acknowledge that he had never ceased thinking about her, when he had allowed time to erase the clearness of her gaze, that untouched look she had as though she had never been in love.

Looking at her now as she approached him gracefully, he was recalling the first time he had seen her. Then as now he was deeply conscious of a pulse beating at the base of his strong brown throat, a stirring sense of adventure, that all too familiar sensation he had experienced whenever he had faced a new challenge like new horizons to explore or a pretty woman to be wooed.

Meeting his half insolent, half probing glance, Rachelle felt the colour rising to her face in a rosy tide.

'Haven't been looking for me by any chance, have you?' he asked in a maddening lazy way which alerted her to the iron will beneath.

'No, but I know someone who has—Nancy. I met her just now,' she replied, halting at the foot of the steps.

He smiled, and Rachelle felt her heart lurch. It made a big difference to his dark sardonic face, although it did not reach his eyes, those deep grey disturbing eyes that made her heart beat alarmingly fast. Suddenly his face sobered. He leaned forward as she mounted the steps and put a lean finger beneath her chin to scan her cheek.

'What's happened to your cheek? Who struck you?' His mouth thinned. 'Where have you been?'

'For a walk.'

'Did Nancy do it?'

'If she did I deserved it.'

He released her chin and raised a brow. 'Nancy isn't usually the slapping kind. Weren't quarrelling over me, were you?'

'You flatter yourself. We got on to the subject of men and I told her that they didn't usually marry women who flaunted their charms blatantly.'

He laughed. 'There are men and men,' he said philosophically. 'Never mind, in the absence of your mother I'll kiss it better.'

His smile was disarming as he bent his head to kiss her cheek lightly.

'Is Pete teasing you, Rachelle?'

Pete straightened and Rachelle was aware of Betty's enquiring gaze on her flushed face as she thrust her arm through her brother's.

'Full of the devil, isn't he?' she prattled on. 'But

he's a nice devil, as I'm sure you've discovered beneath all that veneer of arrogance.' She looked up adoringly at his dark face. 'He used to tease the life out of Mum. I guess he's told you about it.'

Rachelle's blue eyes glittered. 'Yes, you have, haven't you, darling? Thanks for the kiss. I'm returning it.'

She tiptoed to kiss his lean cheek, and felt him stiffen.

'See you at lunch, darling. 'Bye for now.' Rachelle went indoors quickly, chuckling at the expression on his face. What a change to see him taken aback for once.

On her way indoors she met Geoff. 'Seen Betty?' he asked.

'On the veranda with Pete. Anything between you two—or shouldn't I ask?'

Geoff grinned. 'You can ask,' he said.

She laughed. 'All right, tell me to mind my own business. I approve if it helps.'

Minnie was having her breakfast in bed. Rachelle found her sitting up with a tray in front of her.

'Enjoying yourself?' she asked, sitting down on the bed. 'You were fast asleep when I looked in earlier, so I went for a walk.'

'So I believe,' her mother said dryly. 'And Pete was out with Geoff and Betty.' She paused, coffee in hand. 'Do you think Geoff could be serious?'

Rachelle shrugged. 'Your guess is as good as mine.'

Minnie drank the last of her coffee. 'I shouldn't imagine Pete's parents being pleased if he is. After all, he hasn't anything to support a wife.'

'Plenty of couples start from scratch.'

Minnie shuddered. 'I'll have a talk with him.'

'Please, Mother, don't interfere. You could send

him right into her arms if you object. Go along with them and everything will be fine.'

Minnie pursed her lips. 'I went along with you and look what's happened! Does Geoff know how it is between you and Pete?'

Rachelle said quickly, 'No, of course not. I don't want Betty to know.'

'Why not?'

'For Pete. He would hate his people to know that he's failed marriagewise as well as in his present venture. His father wanted him to stay on at the ranch, but Pete wanted to make his own way.'

Minnie considered this. 'So you're going to put on an act, make believe all's well between you. Is that it?'

Rachelle nodded with apprehension. 'You'll have to help me,' she said.

Minnie said blandly, 'In what way?'

'You know ... If I'm in a tight corner with Pete.'

'Do you expect to be?'

Rachelle said helplessly, 'You never know with Pete.'

'I'll do my best,' her mother promised.

Directly after lunch Pete left, taking Minnie with him to the drilling field. She had expressed a wish to go there, but Rachelle had kept silent. In the afternoon Geoff and Betty went in the car Geoff had bought to help him on his travels. Usually he only stayed in one place long enough to earn enough money to tide him over for the next six months.

Rachelle spent the afternoon writing letters to her grandfather and friends. Minnie came in around four, limping, having turned her ankle over while going round the drilling site with Pete.

'I don't blame you for leaving a place like this. It's

positively barbaric!' she groaned.

She sank down into a chair in Rachelle's room and eased off her shoes.

Rachelle looked down at the scraps of leather and straps which her mother had taken off her small feet.

'You're hardly equipped to go trudging around an oilfield, Mother,' she said on a chuckle. 'Your ankle appears to be swollen a bit. I'll get a cold compress.'

'The pleasure is all mine.'

Pete had appeared in the doorway with a bowl of water and a towel over his arm. He knelt down at Minnie's feet and put her foot into the water. Rachelle looked down at the dark head as he took a bandage from his pocket and soaked it. She wanted to reach out and touch him as a surge of tenderness washed over her. If only he would look at her as he was looking at her mother, with that teasing, mocking look which made him so irresistible.

Minnie mumbled, 'Don't be so nice, Pete. I've been airing my views about this place and they weren't exactly to your taste. Why ever did you choose this kind of life? It's no better than keeping pigs! Everybody wallows in the muck, and think what a mess there'll be if you do strike oil!'

Pete laughed. 'The trouble with you is that you're a snob, my dear mother-in-law.'

Minnie laughed, no whit put out by his frank way of speaking.

'Aren't we all?' She gazed down at her foot almost swallowed up in his brown hand and gave a sigh of bliss as he massaged her ankle gently. 'Mmm, it feels better already.'

They spent some time theorising on the subject of snobbery while Rachelle tried to give all her attention to her letter writing. At last the ankle was bandaged firmly and Pete sat back on his knees with a grin.

'How's that?' he asked.

'Lovely. Let me thank you.' Minnie leaned forward and framing his face with her hands kissed him soundly. Then she ran her fingers through the tousled dark hair and said ruefully, 'Your vitality makes me feel my age.'

He shook his head. 'The worst thing you can do at your age is soul-searching. Forget your age. You're as old as you feel—and, I might add, as beautiful as ever.'

'So are you, you big, bad boy!' Minnie sent a wicked look to Rachelle. 'What are we to do with him, Rachelle?'

'Hmm?' Rachelle bit the end of her pen and lifted an absorbed face. 'What did you say?'

She had heard every word passing between them and she hoped that her obvious preoccupation with her letter fooled Pete, though she doubted it.

Minnie said, 'Forget it. Who are you writing to?'

'Grandpa.'

Pete said, 'Give him my love and ask him when he's going to pay me a visit.'

He rose to his feet with the towel he had used thrown over his shoulder and picked up the bowl of water. His glance at Rachelle was mocking, quizzical.

'There'll be a few friends joining us for dinner this evening—Nancy, Jake and Bill,' he said. 'Sarah will cope.'

Rachelle smiled at him with an effort. In other words, she thought, my help will not be needed.

She said sweetly, 'If there's anything I can do let me know.'

'Sure,' he answered. 'See you later.'

Minnie stared down at her neatly bandaged ankle and sighed.

'You're much too offhand with the man, my pet,' she said. 'Why not soften a bit? You could get him eating out of your hand.'

Rachelle snorted. 'Pete will never eat out of anyone's hand. Even Nancy will have to toe the line with him.'

Minnie smiled as though at some secret thought. 'I can imagine nothing nicer than toeing the line with your husband,' she murmured, and slid a sly look at her daughter. 'Maybe Nancy thinks the same.'

Rachelle bit her lip. 'I'm writing to Grandpa. Do you want to write a little postscript?'

Rachelle was looking in her wardrobe for her dress when the tap came on her door. She had the dress over her arm and was bending down for her evening shoes on the floor of the wardrobe when the door opened and closed to silence.

Slowly she turned round, an enchanting figure in lace bra and panties, her face scarlet.

'You might have knocked!' she exclaimed angrily, holding up the dress in front of her.

Pete said, 'I did. I don't know what you're so het up about. I've seen you undressed before.' Tall and wide-shouldered in the silk tailored shirt, he looked fresh and very masculine as his mouth quirked into a smile.

'I need your help,' he said, 'in putting on my tie. I had a little accident, cut my thumb.'

The tie was around his neck and he held up the bandaged thumb. Hastily Rachelle put on the dress, hooked it up the side and came to him. In that moment she could have walked right into his arms, for he looked so like the way he used to when they were first married. There was a mocking glint in his grey eyes, tolerant humour in the upward curve of his mouth ...

Rachelle ignored the ache in her heart and found to her surprise that her fingers did not fumble. All the same, those few brief moments breathing in his masculine fragrance were an ordeal. When a second knock came on the door and a head popped round it, Rachelle received it like a lifeline.

It was Betty. She drew back in confusion. 'Sorry, Rachelle, I thought you were alone. I'll come back later.'

'Come in,' Rachelle invited. 'Since when have you been shy of your own brother?' Stepping back to look at her handiwork, she smiled up at him. 'There you are, darling.'

It was for Betty's benefit that she tiptoed to kiss his chin, only to meet his lips as he bent his head in that moment in mock acknowledgement. Quickly recovering, Rachelle addressed Betty.

'Did you want to see me?' she asked with a warm smile. 'You can speak in front of Pete. We have no secrets from each other—have we, darling?'

Pete made no reply. He looked cool and expectant, and as Rachelle's blue eyes met his she was sure he was enjoying the situation.

Betty looked sweet and shy in a flowered dress which set off her youthful prettiness.

'Actually, Rachelle,' Betty began coming further into the room, 'it was your opinion I wanted. You see ...' She hesitated, saw that neither of them were going to speak and went on. 'Well,' she gave a nervous little laugh, 'Geoff has asked me to marry him, and I wondered what his mother will say. I know she's very fond of him—he's told me.'

'Of course she is. She'd be a bad mother if she wasn't,' Rachelle answered. 'Congratulations. I'm so glad!'

There was faint malice in Pete's smile. 'Congratulations on joining the family,' he drawled, and put his arm around his sister's shoulders, as he bent his head to kiss her cheek.

Betty drew in her lip to moisten it and looked at Rachelle.

'So you think it will be all right where your mother is concerned?'

Rachelle laughed and went to kiss her cheek. 'Of course! There is one thing,' she added. 'While Geoff is a dear, he's also footloose and fancy free at the moment. In other words, he's out of a job.'

Betty brightened. 'Oh, that's no problem. He'll go back to his job at the ranch.' She looked absurdly happy. 'I do hope we shall be as happy as you and Pete are.'

Pete let this pass in silence, then he said, 'No one can wish you more happiness than I do. As for Geoff, I've always had a respect and liking for him because he likes adventure and earning his way like I do.' He gestured deprecatingly. 'On the other hand, no one can hope to achieve the happiness one sees in another couple. Marriage has to be worked on just like any other partnership. Material matters loom largely, like icebergs menacing the calm existence. Am I being too boring?'

Rachelle gave him a prefabricated smile. 'I'm sure you are, darling. Don't frighten the girl. What he's trying to say, Betty, is that marriage is like life, you only get out of it what you put into it. I suppose Geoff has gone to see Mother?'

Minnie took her son's engagement better than

Rachelle had expected. During dinner that evening she maintained her discreet friendly smile, disarming even Betty. Pete kept things in a party mood by being his usual self-assured, urbane self, saying the right thing at the right time, and welcoming Jake, Bill and Nancy with warmth.

Nancy kept a low profile, in a black dress moulded to her curves, and Rachelle played the part of hostess with admirable calm. Once or twice she used endearments when talking to Pete with the feeling that it was expected of her as the loving wife. She only hoped uneasily that she was not overdoing it, while Pete, apart from raising his eyebrows, took it all in his stride.

He filled glasses and saw to his guests until Sarah came in with the first course of the meal. Toasts to the engaged couple were drunk and the conversation was lively. Rachelle sipped wine, ate and laughed when it was expected of her. But her nerves felt raw and Nancy's rather loud laugh grated more than usual.

The meal over, Pete handed round cigarettes and cigars. Nancy accepted her cigarette with a smouldering look at his dark face. Rachelle sat back in her chair while he leaned across her to light Nancy's cigarette. She saw the lean hardness of his firm jaw, the thick black lashes which in spite of his height and broadness made him look boyish and endearing, and her heart went out to him.

For a brief moment his gaze was locked with Nancy's and Rachelle quivered at the hidden meaning in it. Then he did something that took her quite by surprise. He lighted a cigarette and put it between her lips. Rachelle almost dropped it.

He gave a crooked grin at the surprise in her blue eyes.

'Calm your nerves,' he said in an undertone for her ears alone.

Nancy had seen the gesture and transferred her look of venom from them to the young lovers, Geoff and Betty, who had eyes only for each other.

'Why come all this way to announce your engagement when you knew it would happen in any case?' she drawled in hard metallic tones.

Geoff, seated opposite to her at the table with Betty by his side, said with a grin, 'Love is a most unpredictable thing. It can come when you least expect it.'

Nancy blew a line of cigarette smoke into the air and said with bored insolence, 'Unpredictable to a man maybe, but not to a woman. Take Betty—I'd say she came here with the intention of roping you in as a husband.'

Rachelle was aware of Betty's embarrassment, and smiled at her flushed face.

'I bet you did just that whether you intended to or not,' she said with a wink. 'Why not give poor Nancy a few pointers on how to catch her man?'

Everyone laughed goodnaturedly. 'Yes, do. Nancy has some good pointers.' This from Jake.

'Pig!' Nancy snarled.

Pete cringed theatrically. 'Never mind, Nancy,' he said tolerantly. 'Who knows, you might be the next to be married.'

Nancy gave him a long speculative look from beneath curling lashes. 'Who wants marriage anyway?' she said scornfully. 'You and Rachelle are a case in point. You had to part in the end to get yourselves sorted out.'

Rachelle went red, then white. She felt Nancy's hatred, saw the amber eyes gleaming with malice, and

the girl's white pointed teeth showing in a smile that
was no smile. Nancy gave no quarter.

'Don't look so upset, Rachelle,' Nancy purred. 'You
haven't fooled a soul.'

Rachelle's tones were cold, incisive. 'What are you
babbling about? You're wrong, definitely wrong.'

There was silence while they glared at each other
like two opponents armed to the teeth—accusation,
denial. Rachelle clenched her hands and dropped her
cigarette. She was vaguely aware of Pete picking it up
and putting it on an ash tray.

She wanted to yell at him, 'Speak, can't you, or don't
you know which of us to side with?' But she knew well
enough whom he would side with. At last she spoke,
with a calm dignity drawn from her inner strength.

'It seems to me, Nancy, that you need a holiday
yourself to sort things out,' she said coolly. 'You're
certainly confused, and I think you owe Pete and myself an apology.'

There was an uncomfortable silence during which
Pete inhaled from his cigar.

'Rachelle is right, Nancy. You owe us an apology,'
he said quietly.

Nancy's eyes were burning narrow strips of amber,
her mouth a scarlet line, and an angry stain reddered
her cheekbones.

Sulkily, she admitted, 'I've only voiced what others
have been thinking, and I ...'

'Nancy ...' Pete began on a warning note.

She looked at him, realising that she had gone too
far. Gradually her eyes became serene and impersonal
again and her lips smiled as though at some secret
thought.

'I apologise if I was wrong,' she said very softly.

Pete's grey eyes were tempered steel. 'That won't do, Nancy. You will apologise to my wife, and also to Geoff and my sister for attempting to spoil their evening. As a guest in my house you either use your manners or you leave.'

It was Minnie who broke the tension. 'For goodness' sake, Nancy,' she cried, 'pull yourself together! There are times when we all say and do things that are completely out of character. I'm sure you aren't the first person to apologise. We've all had to do it at some time or another in our lives.'

It looked at first as if Nancy was going to refuse. But she apologised with an ill grace and hurried from the table. A few minutes later the sound of her car was heard as she left. The rest of the evening went in an uncomfortable series of masklike duties for Rachelle. She smiled at Geoff, laid a caressing hand on Betty's shoulder and watched them go out on to the veranda.

Then Jake was beside her, leaving Pete talking to Minnie and Bill in the lounge.

'I admired you immensely this evening,' he whispered. 'Against Nancy's churlishness you were sweet and very beautiful. As I said before, you're like a queen. I could go for you in a big way.'

Rachelle drew back. 'Please, Jake,' she sighed, 'not you as well! Why must you spoil the evening? Was it like this while I was away?'

He shrugged. 'Pete did very little entertaining as far as I know. The boys came to play cards occasionally and we all went to Nancy's for parties. What Pete did in between I couldn't say.'

The dark eyes roved her face, the frank enchantment of it, but Rachelle's thoughts had harked back to the scene at the table earlier—Pete's obvious reluctance to bring Nancy's accusations into the open, to contradict them.

Perhaps Pete sensed the strain she was under, because he began to ask her about her sojourn over the water and what things were like there. When the party broke up Jake and Bill left first, then Minnie went to her room. Geoff and Betty had gone for a stroll before retiring, while Rachelle went to the kitchen to see if Sarah needed any help in clearing away.

Returning to the lounge, she found it empty. All was quiet as she went out on to the veranda. It was a relief to be alone after the events of the evening. Her first reaction when Pete had brought her to the bungalow had been a poignant one. It was their first home together, temporary, but a home which she had furnished, and loved. That feeling was no longer there, and something antagonistic was in its place—something aloof—strangely hurtful. Somehow it rejected her, gave her the feeling of being an interloper.

High above her the sliver of moon was veiled in the wide, velvety dark blue sky. The aroma of a cigar floated towards her and she saw the glow of it as Pete stood, a silent figure, with his back to her gazing out into the distance. Was he relieved to be on his own or was he thinking about Nancy?

As if in answer to her thoughts she saw someone join him. Her coat was around her shoulders ... She listened to their voices as their figures closed in together, and a dread feeling of crisis curled around her heart like a cold hand. Nancy had come back. Had they arranged it or could she have returned to make her peace with Pete? Rachelle shivered in the night air and closed her eyes. Somehow she was back in her room where she prepared mechanically for bed. She stood at her window for a long time without the light on wondering if Pete and Nancy were still out there, then slid into bed.

The room was not quite dark. It was filled with warm secretive shadows, tantalising shadows of the past ... of Pete drawing her into his arms, his grey eyes almost black in his need for her. Her dreams were shattered by the sound of someone entering the room.

Pete was in his dressing gown. He came across to the bed. His face in the shadows was tanned, lean, austere with grey eyes that once were filled with laughter. Now they looked at her searchingly. Sitting down on the bed to face her, he said,

'I thought you would have waited to say goodnight. I'm sorry about what happened. It kind of spoiled the evening.'

Rachelle pushed herself up in bed and reminded herself that he had come straight from Nancy's arms.

'I'm not as naïve as you think,' she told him huskily. 'Did you really expect me to wait until your rendezvous with Nancy was over?'

'What rendezvous?'

She stared at him, and pushed the hair from her hot forehead.

'I saw you both just now. I was on the veranda when you met.'

Quite unperturbed, he said, 'You saw Nancy arrive?'

'Just like that,' she mocked him. 'And I suppose you were speechless with surprise?'

'If you mean did I expect her, I didn't.'

Rachelle's blue eyes blazed with anger. 'So convenient, wasn't it, for you to be standing there when she arrived, after the guests had left.'

'What are you getting at? It would be such an easy

way out for you, wouldn't it, if I had an affair with Nancy?'

Rachelle should have been warned by the fury gaining momentum in his face, but she was beyond caring.

'Easy? You bet it would! Why don't you be honest and admit that she's your kind? That you want to marry her?'

Their gaze held, fused together in anger, then Rachelle retreated a little as the dark intent face hardened. Pete reached out then and put his hands on her shoulders. For several seconds her heart stopped as she thought he was going to do her an injury, so dark was his anger.

But he was pushing her down on the bed, his hand moving from her shoulder to the slenderness of her throat to force her head back. When his lips came down in a savage kiss, he felt her tremble.

Rachelle was dazed and shattered. It was like being swallowed in the heat of a fiery furnace, pain and ecstasy together. She had neither the will nor the strength to resist.

CHAPTER SEVEN

RACHELLE awoke from deep blissful slumber to stretch luxuriously in answer to a knock on the door. Her mother came in looking very youthful in a pretty pastel pink wrap, but the lines on her face were more pronounced.

'I want to talk to you, Rachelle. I'm worried,' she began, then broke off to stare at the obvious dent in the pillow beside her daughter. 'Does that mean ...?'

Rachelle pushed herself up in bed with a tide of colour mounting slowly under her skin.

'Don't jump to conclusions, Mother,' she said. 'I went to bed alone last evening. What happened afterwards was something beyond my control.'

Minnie sat down on the bed, put her own problems on one side for a moment and allowed herself a twinkle.

'Let me guess,' she said wickedly. 'Pete decided to take matters into his own hands and claim his conjugal rights. Good for him!'

If Rachelle's lips were expressive, so were the bright blue eyes which now evaded her mother's.

'We ... we had a blazing row,' she admitted with difficulty. 'I don't want to discuss it.'

The twinkle went, and Minnie's eyes widened in disbelief.

'You mean you haven't made it up?' she demanded.

'To be honest, I don't know. What are you worried about? It's Geoff, isn't it? You resent his engagement to Betty?'

Minnie's lips formed a stubborn line. 'Stop prevaricating! I want to know what happened between you and Pete last evening.'

Rachelle borrowed her stubbornness. 'Really, Mother,' she exclaimed resentfully, 'there are some things that are sacred between husband and wife!'

'Come off it,' Minnie said bluntly. 'You'll be saying next that Pete didn't come to your room last night.'

'I told you I came to bed alone. Pete was out,' she insisted.

'Don't tell me he didn't come to your room. I saw him.'

Rachelle stared at her. 'You were spying on me?'

'Of course I wasn't. I came to talk to you about Geoff and as I left my room I saw Pete coming in here to you in his robe. He didn't come out, so I waited.'

'So what? I don't want to talk about it—besides, it doesn't concern you, does it?'

Minnie sat up straight, saying indignantly, 'It concerns me a great deal. Either you've made it up with Pete or you haven't.'

'We haven't made it up. From what I can make of last night, Pete was frustrated. He ... he just needed a woman, that's all.'

Minnie looked down at the slender fingers plucking unhappily at the bedcover. The golden band on her finger gleamed no less bright than the light in the grey eyes as she spoke.

'I don't believe that. Pete isn't that kind of man. He can discipline himself not to follow his baser instincts.'

'He met Nancy last night,' said Rachelle flatly. 'I saw them. I was on the veranda after helping Sarah in the kitchen. Pete was there smoking a cigar and Nancy joined him.'

Minnie looked startled. 'What happened then?'

'I don't know. I came to bed.'

'Did you tell Pete you'd seen him with Nancy?'

'Yes. He denied that it was prearranged.'

Minnie hugged her knees. 'Do you think that little scene at the dinner table could have been arranged between them so that Nancy could go home and sneak back later to see Pete?' she asked thoughtfully.

Rachelle drew in a deep unhappy breath. She was torn by inner conflict. It just did not make sense. She was ready to believe the worst of Pete, yet she wanted him with a dreadful and nostalgic longing and dreaded meeting him again. I've made a mess of things, she thought drearily ... I was unreasonable, demanding the best things in life, material comforts ... that aren't really the best things after all. The best things are being loved and wanted and giving intead of having.

Last evening she had given way to Pete's lovemaking like someone starved of love. It had to be one thing or the other: her career, or life with Pete if he would have her back. And what kind of life would that be if he took her back without love? She sat very still thinking things out, her bare arms and shoulders pale as cream, gleaming richly like the pale brown lights in her damp, curling hair.

She shivered and faced reality. 'I don't know what Pete had planned or has planned,' she answered dully. 'I only know he would have been here beside me now if he'd wanted a reconciliation.'

Minnie said hopefully, 'Maybe he has to see Nancy first to tell her what he proposes to do.'

Rachelle shook her head. 'Not Pete. He asks no one's permission for anything he does.'

Her mother smiled. 'Then that settles it. I not only get my daughter back, I have my son back as well.'

'How do you make that out?'

'Your marriage with Pete has broken up. Right? Then all you have to do is tell him so and his sister too. Tell Betty that as a family we're better left alone. Neither Geoff nor you are capable of keeping a lasting relationship with anyone. Then we can all go back home.'

Rachelle thrust her legs out of bed and reached for her wrap.

'You're talking nonsense, Mother, and you know it. If I go back I shall have a flat of my own. As for Geoff, he won't be at home any more than he is now. He'll just continue travelling around the world until he becomes a hobo or something else just as humiliating. Betty is just the girl for him and he has a chance of a good future with her at the ranch. I refuse to discuss it any more. I'll see you at breakfast.'

But when Minnie had gone Rachelle put on her swimsuit and decided to go to the creek for a swim to think things out. Sarah came in with a cup of tea as she was looking out her beach bag.

'Going out?' she queried, setting down the tray. 'I thought I'd bring you a cuppa. Pete went out early. Going to the creek for a swim? Well, let's hope it sharpens your appetite.'

Sarah was ready for gossip, but Rachelle sipped her tea and was off. Much as she liked Sarah, there was an aching need to be alone. The water rippled softly over her limbs in the quiet of the creek. Rachelle closed her mind to all things unpleasant and gave herself up to relaxing her body in the water.

She had towelled herself briskly behind rocks and was dressed when she heard someone approaching. It was Nancy.

Rachelle shook her half dried hair back and turned a glowing face.

'Hello,' she said. 'Still looking for Pete?'

Nancy smiled insolently. 'No, I'm looking for you. Well, not exactly looking, since I didn't know you were here, but I was on my way to your place to see you.'

'Home from home, would you say?' Rachelle murmured sarcastically. 'Only now the mistress is back.'

'True, and we want you back like a hole in the head. When are you leaving?'

'Now that's a point. I'll have to think about it.'

Nancy said amiably, 'I think we should have a little talk to our mutual benefit.'

'Really?' said Rachelle coldly as she combed out her hair.

'Why so unfriendly, sweetie?' The amber eyes mocked. 'All right,' hastily, 'I know I spoke out of turn last night, but I did apologise. What do you want me to do grovel?'

Rachelle felt a sweep of cold anger. Not wanting to quarrel, however, she was silent. Her aggressiveness was a protection against the other girl's animosity.

'What is it, Nancy?' she asked impatiently.

'Like I said, a talk. We won't be interrupted here like we would be at the house. What exactly do you plan to do?'

'About what?'

'About Pete, of course.'

Rachelle smoothed her hair into place and replaced things she had been using in her beach bag.

'I don't think I feel like discussing things this morning. To begin with I've had no breakfast and I'm feeling rather drowsy after ... last night.' Her blue eyes twinkled into the amber ones. 'Pete is a passionate man.'

Nancy looked thunderstruck. Her mouth thinned and her eyes hardened until the pupils were dark points in the amber. With shaking fingers she withdrew a packet of cigarettes from her pocket and lighted one. She puffed furiously and Rachelle waited.

'I think you ought to know,' Nancy said at last with some measure of calmness, 'I returned to your place last night to meet Pete. If he made love to you later it was because of the frustration of not being able to be with me. I was there by appointment.'

The words were deadly weapons against any reassurance Rachelle had from her own courage. Her
head high, her blue eyes, steady and unafraid, roved
disdainfully over the other girl's smilingly malicious
face. She had never had any time for Nancy, her
brazenness, her denial of everything feminine except
where her body was concerned. The girl had one saving grace: she spoke the truth as she saw it. She
plunged where angels feared to tread, but it made it
easier to understand her.

She smiled almost pityingly. 'Pete told me you'd
called. I saw you from the terrace.'

Nancy gaped. The cigarette clinging to her lower lip
was taken slowly in her fingers, and she threw her head
back to evade the smoke. Rachelle gazed upon the long
column of her throat, the red hair, and decided that
Nancy was some girl if only she would get her priori-
ties right.

'Oh well, you'll know I'm speaking the truth, then.
We can go on from there. As I said before, Pete made
love to you as a substitute for me. As you say, he's
passionate, as I remember. He makes love divinely,
doesn't he?' Malice sharpened the amused chuckle.
'Small wonder you're tired this morning.'

Rachelle quivered inwardly at her crudeness. She
had always regarded the intimate side of marriage as
sacred, to be known only to the couple concerned. She
would never have dreamed of saying to anyone else
what she had said to Nancy. She was beyond words.

Nancy was smiling at her pale face. 'Cigarette?' she
said, and her hand went to her pocket.

Rachelle shook her head gravely, horrified, repelled
by what Nancy had said. Her enchanting face ex-

pressed rapt attention and Nancy was goaded into a furious jealous reaction.

'Don't sit there looking like God's gift to some glossy magazine cover!' she cried. 'If you think that sitting around looking beautiful is going to get Pete back, you're nuts. I've told you, it's me he wants. In any case, everybody around here knows it, even Sarah. If Pete were to have you back now all his friends would say he'd welshed on me. As you're not altogether stupid I'm sure you'll see what I mean. Why don't you go before you're humiliated further?'

'What a dreadful creature you are!' Rachelle's clear voice rang on the morning air. 'How dare you discuss anything so intimate as my life with Pete! You're trying to belittle a man who would be better off without either of us. You can't arrange other people's lives like a game of chess. Please go, and leave me alone.'

Rachelle sat for a long time staring into space. She drew her knees up and clasped them under the shade of an old arched tree. There was nothing to keep her at the bungalow. Geoff would be leaving soon with Betty and her mother would soon tire of being in a part of the world so different from her surroundings back home. She felt encompassed by the unkind ways of fate. Her thoughts wandered into delectable avenues as she pushed back the soft brown hair from her face.

How long she sat Rachelle never knew. She was interrupted in her thoughts by someone dropping down beside her and looked round to see Jake Denver.

'Hello there. Penny for them,' he teased. 'Nancy said I would find you here.'

Rachelle glanced at dark eyes which were embarrassingly absorbing her.

'For wide open spaces, I find these extraordinarily

crowded,' she told him dryly. 'I was about to go and have breakfast. Shouldn't you be at work?'

'As it happens I am. I . . .'

'You called along to see Rachelle. Another rendezvous, is it?'

Pete stood there glaring down on them. Rachelle saw to her surprise that he looked pale beneath his tan. His expression of contempt sent a noise like the roaring of water in her ears; she had the feeling of being entirely on her own with only Pete in the whole universe. Jake was on his feet.

'Sorry, Pete. I was just on my way,' he said.

'That's all right, Jake. Push off.'

The sparkling slivers of silver glancing on the water in the creek were as steely as Pete's grey eyes as Rachelle pushed back her shining hair to get to her feet. The next moment his brown hand was on her shoulder, pushing her down again. Then he dropped down beside her.

'Not yet,' he said. 'I want to talk to you.'

Rachelle watched him draw up one of his long legs and rest an arm along his knee as he stared at the creek.

She said, 'I didn't arrange to meet Jake here. Nancy was here not long ago. She could have told him I was at the creek.' She stared at his unyielding profile, at the set line of his jaw. 'I'm speaking the truth.'

He said without expression, 'Jake is always hanging around since you've come back.'

She lifted her chin. 'Since when has he been forbidden to speak to me?'

'It's the way he does it. He never expected me to come looking for you.'

'What of it? With Nancy behaving as though I had no right to come back it's nice to have one friend around.'

Pete said coldly, 'Jake isn't exactly the kind of man I would want my wife to be friends with. There's no question of platonic friendship between you two and you know it. Besides, you've been seeing Jake since you came here.'

'That's a lie!' she flared.

'You met him on the first morning at the bungalow. You just couldn't wait to see him. Was he the reason you left?'

His eyes glittered and he spoke with a deadly quietness. By now Rachelle was quivering with anger.

'You know very well he wasn't.'

'I know he's always had a soft spot for you and that Nancy is worried about you meeting him.'

'Poor Nancy! She's so worried about me being with you. If she's been hinting at anything between Jake and myself your own sense ought to tell you that it isn't true. Would I run away from one prospector for oil to link myself up to another?'

'Sounds convincing,' with irony. 'All right, let's go on from here. At least we can talk without anyone butting in here. No one will know anything about our argument if it turns into one. After all, you have a brother and mother here and I dare say Betty would be on your side too.' Sarcasm deepened his voice. 'You have enough supporters if you need them.'

Rachelle quivered inwardly, trying to see in him the man of the previous night who had held her in his arms ...

'There's nothing to discuss,' she said heavily.

'Look, we have to talk. Things can't go on like this. I won't keep you long,' Pete promised. 'Sarah says you haven't had any breakfast.'

'Nice of you to be so concerned!'

'I'm concerned about both of us,' he stated in clipped tones. 'The situation is ridiculous. I've kept it dark and I mean to go on doing so until Betty has gone. I won't have my sister going home to my folks and telling them I've failed in everything I set out to do, including keeping a wife by my side.'

Her head was lowered. 'There's no chance of that. When Betty and Geoff leave Mother is sure to want to go with them. She'll put things right by saying we're only having separate jobs until things get better.'

'And what do you propose to do if that happens?'

'Go back home.'

'This is your home, here with your husband. You're my wife. You're a coward, Rachelle,' he jeered softly. 'You say one thing and mean another.'

The colour in her face rushed to the roots of her hair.

'If you're referring to last night, what chance had I got against you?'

'None, when I take hold of you. But I don't want you that way. What happened last night won't happen again unless we're both of the same mind. All I ask is that we behave like a normal married couple for the next few days.'

Rachelle was silent. She remembered the faint mockery in his voice as he had taken her against her will the previous night into his arms, the slight roughness and the magic. His expression was unreadable. How she longed to get beneath that impersonal front! He was like a rock, well disciplined in all his movements. She was no match for him.

'I can manage that,' she admitted at last.

Pete was looking on the sparkling water in the creek. 'Nice spot here to think and meditate. This is a wonderful country. It's also something we've shared.' His tones held a trace of a smile. 'Surprising how everyone has accepted you back as if you've never been away.'

Rachelle lowered her eyes as he turned towards her. 'I'm not the same person who went away.' She stopped hugging her knees and straightened her legs, supporting herself with splayed hands. It was a terrible temptation to tell him that she had left hating him and returned loving him. But she held the words back. There was no way of knowing how close he and Nancy had become during her absence. If only he would tell her that he loved her, ask her to come back!

'We all change as we grow older in some ways.' His glance was purely speculation. 'I haven't seen much evidence of that sense of humour that used to bubble up inside you. Maybe I've lost a little myself. You're feeling happier, though, about this new scheme of yours, aren't you?'

A little huskily she answered, 'As yet it's an unknown quantity, so I can't feel entirely happy about it.' She cleared her throat. 'I try not to dwell on it ... not to expect too much. That's why it was so good to go home and share Grandpa's problems. I had no time to dwell on anything else.'

'You mean dwell on your husband?'

'Anything.'

Pete's tones were dry. 'Thanks for including me in all and sundry. It might interest you to know that you're in my thoughts quite often. Sometimes those thoughts drive me into positive action.'

Like last night, she thought, and her body went hot all over at the memory.

'I'm sorry ... I know you share my disappointment at the way things have turned out,' she began.

He covered the hand nearest to him with strong fingers.

'Don't blame marriage for our failure to see eye to eye. Marriage never fails. It's the people who take it on who just aren't big enough to go along with it. They have to put the blame for their own inadequacy on something. Falling in love with the right person is the right start as long as you never lose sight of the fact that you have to prove to be the right partner for that person.' His smile rocked her heart. 'Too bad I'm setting you off on thinking about things you would rather forget, and I'm going to stop another train of thought too, something that's bothered me.'

Rachelle felt the warmth of his hand over hers sending vibrations through her body. Her first reaction to draw her own hand away had been too weak to insist. With an inward helpless feeling she knew that, though her common sense told her to be firm, her treacherous heart was capable of taking over each time he touched her.

'What is it?' she queried, head lowered.

'Your grandfather. I have a strange conviction that things are going to happen.'

Horror widened her blue eyes. 'You mean he's going to die?'

Pete laughed. 'What a little pessimist you are! I mean Mrs Carne will soon be taking over, if I'm not mistaken.'

Rachelle drew in a breath of pure delight. 'You really think so? It would change everything for Mother. She could sell the house and take a flat if she wanted.'

Her laugh was tinkle of pure delight and he squeezed her hand. Her hair had dried in curly tendrils around her flushed face. She looked fresh, young and clear-eyed with the beauty of youth.

'I don't believe it—you're actually laughing! Come on, let me take you back home while you're still glowing. Besides, I shall have Sarah after me for keeping you from your breakfast.'

With the ease of active muscles Pete was on his feet with little effort to catch hold of her wrists and pull her up on to her feet.

'Grandpa marrying again—how lovely!' she cried, shining up at him.

For heart-burning seconds he looked down into her very blue eyes. His head lowered a little and a light came into his grey eyes which stopped her heart. The next moment it had gone.

Soberly he drawled, 'Let's pray he makes a better job of it than we've done.'

The world around them stood still as their eyes locked. Rachelle's treacherous heart was urging her on to make her peace with him ... to adapt herself to his way of life ... to force herself to accept another world far removed from the one she craved for.

He would not always be struggling in the mire and he would never drag her down to anything degrading other than honest labour. But could she do it not knowing how he felt now towards her? There are times in one's life when opportunities come at the right moment, Rachelle knew. But was this one of them?

Pete broke the spell. He was reaching out to touch her hair and he leaned forward to breathe in its fragrance.

'Hmm, lovely,' he breathed. 'There's fairy gold dust in your hair and it feels like pure silk.'

He laughed a little, took her arm and they began

walking back to the bungalow. He released her after a while and dug his hands into his pockets, strangely silent. Rachelle had never felt less like talking. Already the warm intimacy between them, precious minutes from time that had gone past recall except in memory, were swallowed up in the mists of eternity, and she wanted to die.

Minnie was waiting for them on the veranda of the bungalow. She looked at her daughter impatiently.

'What's all this, roaming around before breakfast?' she demanded. 'Joined a jogging club or something?' Her glance at the beach bag Rachelle carried was baleful. 'I've been waiting for you for ages.'

Pete said, 'Well, she's here now. Behave yourselves, and have a nice day.'

He strolled along to his office and Minnie followed her daughter to the kitchen.

'Sarah is out, gone for provisions. Your breakfast is ready. I'll make coffee,' she said with an ill grace. 'How have you and Pete got on? Sarah asked him to fetch you in for breakfast.'

Rachelle sat down at the table and reached for her fruit juice.

She said, 'What would you say to Grandpa getting married again?'

Minnie spilled the coffee she was spooning out into the percolator.

'Married again?' she echoed. 'To whom? He wasn't at the home long enough to make a lasting relationship with anyone there.'

Rachelle said coolly, 'Mrs Carne, of course. They play chess together and they appear to get on very well. Mind you, it's only a suggestion from Pete.'

'It makes sense,' Minnie conceded. 'That husband

of yours isn't just a handsome face. I wouldn't put it past him to arrange the whole thing. After all, he has let Dad stay in the flat.'

'Well, what do you think?' Rachelle insisted.

'It hasn't happened yet, has it?' Minnie came to the table with the coffee. 'What annoys me is that if Pete can manage anyone else's affairs why doesn't he manage his own better—you for one.'

Rachelle spread butter on a roll. 'I'm not an appendage of Pete, I'm a free agent. Where are Betty and Geoff?'

Minnie had poured out the coffee and added sugar to her own.

'You may well ask. They're as bad as you for disappearing. At least they have a reason, they're in love.'

Rachelle bit hard on the roll now spread with honey. She wanted to scream, so am I in love with my husband. Instead she asked, 'Have they decided yet what they're going to do?'

Minnie lifted her cup daintily. 'Betty wants to marry as soon as possible. Geoff wants to wait. I'm with Geoff,' she stated firmly.

Rachelle laughed helplessly. 'You would! Don't you see that this is a chance for Geoff to make something of himself? Besides, if Grandpa marries again you can sell the house after all. You could even go on a trip around the world or better still go to visit your son when he's settled down.'

Minnie stated dryly, 'Geoff isn't married yet, neither is Dad. Anything done in a hurry rarely has lasting benefits. Strangely enough, I'm more bothered about you at the moment. Now, if you'd make it up with Pete that would complete the picture.'

Rachelle's face was a study of shock and anger.

'Why, that's blackmail! You mean if I do that you'll
go along with everything else?'

Minnie smiled and replenished her cup. 'Something
like that,' she murmured.

Rachelle nearly choked on the rest of her bread roll.
She said threateningly, 'You must see, of course, that
you leave me no alternative other than to tell Geoff to
take Betty home as soon as possible. I will not have you
interfering in his life or mine!'

Minnie siad calmly, 'If I remember right, you asked
me to help you with Pete. Now you're telling me to
keep out. You're a fool, Rachelle. You're letting a good
man go.'

Rachelle's face went red, then white. 'He's gone
already, Mother. He doesn't want me. He asked me
this morning to behave normally as his wife until his
sister goes back home ...' She broke off, seeing the
thoughtful look on her mother's face. 'And don't you
dare interfere between Pete and me!' she threatened. 'I
won't have it. Do you hear?'

Minnie drank her coffee. 'Then I shall go with Betty
and Geoff. I shall want to be at their wedding. I shall
wash my hands of you completely. As for Dad, he can
do as he chooses. I shall certainly not sell the house
until I know what he's going to do.'

As if to emphasise her decision Minnie put her cup
down with a thud and went to her room. Rachelle sat,
taken aback, then she began to smile. Life had its com-
pensations after all. With Geoff, Betty and her mother
gone, there would be no reason for her to stay here.
She could go back home to concentrate on her career
and hunt for a flat.

But there was little joy in the thought of leaving
Pete. She felt clammy, weak, and utterly bereft. The

coffee slid down her throat, a throat blocked by emotions which threatened to choke her. His forceful masculinity, the air of nonchalant grace that was part of his wide-shouldered, narrow-hipped body, had captured her heart for all time. He had strode into her life from wide open spaces and he was striding out of it back to them. She recalled softly lit evenings here in this very room when he came in to greet her. His embrace had been enchanting, his face cool from the outdoors, his mouth on hers warm and urgent as his kiss lingered until she had been out of breath. Her life stretched before her, not widening into adventurous channels with Pete but gradually dwindling into the final acceptance of compromise.

'Hello there!'

Geoff came bursting into the unhappy bubble of her thoughts. He looked fit and glowing with life.

'Any more coffee in the pot?' he asked, taking a chair opposite her at the table.

'Where's Betty?' Rachelle asked as she fetched a cup and saucer.

'Gone to her room to pack. We've been for a run in the car to discuss going back to the ranch. Betty wants to go now. She also wants us to be married when we get there, as soon as we can.' He raised his brows comically at Rachelle's guarded look as she handed him the coffee. 'We don't have to get married, if that's what you are thinking. She thinks I might change my mind.'

Rachelle poured the rest of the coffee in her cup. 'So she isn't sure of you. Do you love her, Geoff?'

'Yes, I adore her, and I know we're right for each other.' He spooned sugar into his cup. 'There are obstacles in the way, though.'

'Like what?'

'Well, I haven't much money at the moment and I won't let her parents help. I want her to wait a while.'

'She will if she has you there at the ranch with her.'

Rachelle's smile was reassuring, but it did not wipe off the worried expression on his pleasant face.

'I know that,' he said. 'There are other obstacles.'

'Do you intend to make a home in this country?' she asked him frankly.

He shrugged. 'Living next to nature is the only way to be happy, I reckon, and you can't get any nearer nature than here in this marvellous country. Once you settle in a city you begin wanting things that become too important. What about you, Rachelle? I bet there are times when you yearn for material things after being brought up among them.'

Rachelle bit her lip. 'Mine isn't a case in point, since I've had breaks in running a beauty salon and going home for a visit,' she prevaricated.

He smiled. 'You look so out of place here. Betty thinks so too. She's been telling Pete he had no right to keep you here.' A pause. 'We've heard rumours about you and Pete,' he went on awkwardly. 'And Nancy set us off believing them after that scene at dinner the other evening.'

Rachelle had been half prepared for this and said resolutely, 'Nancy has her eye on Pete, so naturally she'll make mischief. Also, small communities thrive on gossip. They have nothing else to do. Surely it's enough for you to see that Pete and I are together?' Hastily, she changed the subject. 'How do you feel about Mother going with you when you return to the ranch?'

Geoff frowned. 'Has she suggested it?'

She nodded. 'Stated it, would be more like it. She wants to be at your wedding.'

'She does?' Geoff suddenly looked brighter. 'I thought she was against me marrying Betty.'

'She is. But then Mother wants to keep you to herself, you know that. She doesn't think there's anyone good enough for you. However, she's coming to terms with the idea of you and Betty. To be fair, Mother was upset about Grandpa. Now he's likely to get settled I rather think she feels a need to shed all responsibility of her family and move house into a flat.'

He gestured. 'That's the way it is with families. They cause problems. Take Pete's.'

'Pete's family? What about Pete's family?' Rachelle asked curiously.

He leaned back in his chair and eyed her quizzically.

'How much has Pete told you about his family?' he asked.

'Not much.'

'You know that he fell out with his father? That the old man wanted to take him into partnership on the ranch and that Pete wanted to start off his own bat by buying that partnership?'

She nodded. 'Something like that.'

'Thereby hangs a tale. You see, if I go back with Betty and we marry right away, her father might feel obliged to take me into partnership. We get on well together because, like Pete, I'm not afraid of hard work, which is why I'm not going to marry until I have enough money to put down on a place of my own.'

Rachelle was impressed. Her brother had certainly improved in his attitude to life.

She said, 'Good for you! At least Betty will know

you aren't marrying her for the advantages her family might bring.'

He grinned. 'I never thought of that. I'm glad Mother wants to go with us to the ranch. I only wish that Pete would agree to bring you,' he added. 'His parents miss him.'

Rachelle shook her head. 'Pete has a mind of his own. I can't see him going back home yet. He's too proud to go back and admit defeat.'

Geoff said soberly, 'I'm afraid he won't get very far here as regards striking oil. Too much water about, according to the experts.'

Rachelle lifted her chin. 'I don't agree with you. Pete is no fool. I'm with him all the way. He's the most honest and dependable man I know.'

Goodness, what am I saying? she thought. I'm not going along with him at all. I've deserted him in his hour of need. I never saw it this way before.

Geoff approved boyishly, 'Glad to hear you say that. I hope Betty goes along with me and is just as loyal. There'll be lean times for us, but we'll get through. She's the right girl.'

Rachelle cleared her throat. 'I'm sure she is.'

She had never felt really close to her brother and had regarded him as being selfish in the past. He had refused any responsibility and had toured the world living on a shoestring and sending home for money from time to time when he could not make it. But he had matured and seemed ready to settle down. What he had told her about Pete had disturbed her, but there was nothing she could do about it.

Geoff cut into her thoughts. 'What's this about Grandpa settling down?'

She told him about Pete fetching him from the old

folks' home and installing him in the flat in London, and all about Mrs Carne the housekeeper.

He said sheepishly, 'Mother wrote mentioning a flat and selling the house. I told her to go ahead.'

'You never gave a thought to Grandpa, did you?' Rachelle accused.

'No, I didn't. You have a good man in Pete.' He looked at his wristwatch. 'I'll go to have a word with Mother.'

Slackly, Rachelle rose to her feet and carried the used dishes to the sink to wash them. It seemed that the pattern of her life was taking on a shape of its own without her assistance. Soon Geoff, Betty and her mother would be gone and there would be no excuse for her to stay on. The sweet intimate relationship she had enjoyed with Pete that had held a promise of joyful fulfilment was no more.

Even if she was willing to come back to him Pete did not want her. He had learned to live without her; that was the truth and she had to accept it. Unwittingly, she had broken the bonds between them herself and to her utter desolation had discovered her love for him in doing so. The dishes washed, Rachelle stood in the kitchen like one lost. No use going in to see her mother yet. Geoff would be talking to her and Betty would be packing.

Then she saw it perched on the top of a cupboard, the toy panda Pete had brought her back on the occasion he had gone away for spares for the drilling. Because she had wanted no reminders of him when she had left the panda had been left behind. Carrying a chair to the cupboard, Rachelle slipped off her shoes, stood on the chair seat and reached for the toy.

The next moment she was hugging it against her.

The cold plastic nose seemed very real against her soft
cheek.

'What a reunion!' Pete scoffed from behind her.

Rachelle started violently and would have fallen off
the chair had he not put up his hands to steady her.

Her face flushed, she said crossly, 'You shouldn't
sneak up on me like that!'

'I didn't. You were too taken up with the panda. I'm
surprised you didn't take it with you.'

Her anger faded and her eyes filled with tears. She
wanted to say, like a fool I left everything behind that
I loved, but no words came. Then Pete's hands were on
her trim waist and he was lifting her from the chair. He
did not release her right away but kept his hands in
their grip. His deep exclamation was unexpected.

'Heavens, you're as light as thistledown! Been on a
diet or something?' He bent his head and looked sideways into her face as she held the panda in one arm.
'You'll eat a good breakfast in the morning if I have to
give it to you myself.'

She said, 'You've been spending too much time with
Nancy. We represent a before and after between us,
don't we? I'll never be like her.'

His hands dropped from her waist. His voice was as
cold as the snows.

'No, you won't, will you?'

If he had slapped her Rachelle could not have felt
the implication of his words more. In the moment of
his arrival she had needed him so much that the desire
to hurt had forced remarks to her lips that would never
have been there before. The warm feel of his hands on
her waist was still there.

He moved the chair from the cupboard back to the
table, and she looked up at him, white-faced.

'I'm sorry, I shouldn't have said that ... about Nancy, I mean. Since I've come back Sarah has been on to me to eat more, and now you ...'

His jaw had hardened slightly. 'Forget it,' he said curtly. 'Have you any idea where Geoff and Betty are and if they'll be in for lunch?'

'They're both here. Has Betty told you she wants to go home with Geoff?'

Pete was busy taking food from the freezer. He said, 'I expected it. After all, they are going to be married.'

Rachelle watched him helplessly. 'What are you doing?' she asked politely.

'Getting lunch. Sarah won't be back until late.'

'I see.' Her heart felt as frozen as the food he was placing on the table. 'Can I help?'

He said coolly, 'Betty will be here. We've become used to being without you. I'm afraid it will be a cold buffet.'

Rachelle flinched as if he had struck her. Her voice wobbled. 'That's ... straight from the shoulder anyway. I thought I was supposed to act like a normal wife?'

Pete looked her straight in the eye. 'In the kitchen, yes. But Betty asked if she could prepare lunch since Sarah will be out.'

'Sorry I intruded,' Rachelle said quietly. At the door she looked down at the panda in her arms. 'I think Mother will go with Geoff and Betty when they leave. Geoff thinks you ought to go home on a visit too. He says your parents miss you.'

Pete presented her with his back as he washed his hands at the sink.

'It isn't possible for me to leave at present. I shall be going home to see the folks one day,' he answered.

Again Rachelle had the awful feeling of being shut out, and the prick of tears behind her eyes grew more pronounced. The next moment she had bumped into someone coming into the kitchen.

'Sorry!' Betty gasped, and stared at the panda in Rachelle's arms. 'You aren't in the family way, are you, Rachelle?' she asked. 'I mean, you aren't starting a nursery?'

Rachelle went red, then white, saw Pete's gaze move to Betty's delighted smile and could almost hear his sarcastic silence.

Pride kept her voice low and steady. 'No. This was a present from Pete many moons ago.'

'Cuddly, isn't he?' said Betty, patting the panda's head. 'I still have my old teddy bear—but don't tell anybody. I'm saving it for my son.' Her smile was warm. 'You don't mind me getting the lunch, do you, Rachelle? Pete said it would be all right.'

'Not at all. You won't mind Mother going with you when you leave, will you?' Rachelle smiled and managed to sound lighthearted. 'She thinks the world of Geoff.'

'It will be fun,' Betty conceded. 'All we need now is for you and Pete to come too.'

'I'm afraid it isn't convenient right now,' Rachelle replied, avoiding Pete's eyes.

'That's right it isn't.' Pete hung up the towel he had used to dry his hands, and said without interest, 'Anything else you need, Betty, for a cold lunch? Most of it is here on the table.'

CHAPTER EIGHT

RACHELLE was taking her dress from the hanger when a peremptory knock came at her door and Pete strode in. He found himself confronted by creamy shoulders, a delightful curved breast, small waist and a neat little bottom. The long slim legs completed a picture that had tormented him through the weeks of her absence. She was in her panties and bra.

His eyes narrowed as she turned to face him. Her whole attitude presented a challenge he found it hard to resist. Deliberately his grey eyes strayed wickedly to her aloof face and then back to her delightful curves. It would serve her right if he hauled her into his arms and had his own way. If he decided to exert his considerable strength she would be as helpless as a baby. He quelled a chuckle as he imagined her outraged fury.

Then he saw that she was not as challenging in her aloofness as she appeared to be. She looked like a defenceless child with her hair pushed back behind her small ears and her face pinkly unhappy. Pete quashed the base emotions she had aroused in him and forgave her. But the wicked little gnome still sat on his shoulder urging him to tease her nervousness.

'Need any help?' he enquired, moving nearer.

His voice was warmly aggressive. Rachelle was too scared to meet his teasing gaze. Slipping on the dress hastily, she demanded, 'What were you doing looking through the keyhole?'

'That's an idea. I think the bathroom keyhole would be more enlightening, don't you?'

He laughed as she gazed up at him in furious incredulity.

'I don't think that's funny,' she snapped, struggling to zip up the back of her dress.

Audaciously, he watched her struggles as he laughed wickedly into her blazing eyes.

'I'm teasing you, but it's your own fault. I'm only a man, after all. I never could resist a challenge, so don't go around needling me. In fact, I'm quite capable of adding up the score between us and taking what's coming to me in one grand gesture. Then we shall be quits and you can go with no hard feelings on my side.'

Rachelle was finding it hard to keep calm while struggling with the stubborn zip on her dress between feeling frightened, humiliated and just a little hurt.

'I don't know what I ever saw in you,' she cried. 'You're the most hateful man I've ever known! Oh ...' this while she struggled unsuccessfully with the zip, 'go away! How dare you come into my room while I'm dressing?'

'Careful now,' he warned. 'You're living dangerously when you dare me.'

He moved in closer and Rachelle stepped back. 'Get out! Do you hear?' she cried.

'What are you afraid of?' He paused with a glint in his eyes and a wicked smile on his lips. 'You have no cause to be afraid of me unless you dare me too far. Let's put things straight here and now. I have no desire to repeat what happened the other night—I'm hoping you'll bear that in mind. I came in to tell you that Betty, Geoff and your mother are leaving in the morning. When they've gone it will be advisable for you to stay on for a few days to give the impression that all is well here.'

The zip came up in her fingers and she dropped her arm to push back her hair.

Trembling, she retorted, 'You needn't be so arrogant about it. I can please myself whether I stay or not. You don't give me much encouragement to.'

'That goes both ways,' he answered grimly, then his voice softened. 'I reckon I've been pretty lenient with you because I have the good sense to control my emotions up to now. But there is a limit and, as a man, I have an unfair advantage over you. Don't goad me into using it, that's all.'

The next moment he had left the room and Rachelle groped her way to sit down on the bed. She felt spent and drained of all emotion. She was beginning to loathe the bungalow, along with everything of the workings that surrounded it. If only it was possible to skip over the next few days to the time she was on her way out of Pete's life! How was she going to bear it?

Rachelle was still shaking when she was ready to go in to dinner that evening. It was knowing that she was going to see Pete again, his presence that bothered her, the ridiculous charade of them playing host and hostess at dinner. Those taunting grey eyes mocked her; he was so sure of himself, his strength. Again she felt the warm flush of anger at the thought of meeting those mocking eyes and knowing that there was nothing she could do about it.

Loneliness began to curdle in her chest, to stay there all through the evening. Sarah was back and there was a pleasing aroma coming from the kitchen as she entered the lounge. They were all there. Geoff and Betty had the look of a couple who had just won a lottery and Minnie, looking chic in midnight blue, was smiling up at Pete, who was offering her a drink.

Murmuring something, Rachelle went to the kitchen, to find Sarah industriously whipping up cream.

'Hello there,' she said without pausing in her whipping. 'I see your panda has gone. Did you take it, Rachelle?'

Rachelle nodded. 'It's in my ... the bedroom,' she answered, sitting down at the kitchen table. 'I don't know why I took it there.'

'I do. You need children. A baby will claim your attention, take your mind off what's going on out there.'

'I'm not sure that's the answer. I don't seem to be sure about anything any more,' Rachelle sighed.

Sarah eyed her kindly. 'Why did you come back, Rachelle?'

'I don't really know. I came with Mother. I'm still going after a career, Sarah.'

'And what makes you think you can make a success of it when only half of you is in it?'

Rachelle said shakily, 'I don't know what you mean.'

Sarah stopped whipping the cream. 'I think you do. You came out here with Pete, leaving part of you behind, the ambitious part. You wanted to have your cake and eat it at the same time.'

Rachelle blushed warmly. 'That isn't true, Sarah, and you know it.'

Sarah went on undaunted. 'What's more, you'll go back leaving half of yourself here. How you can hope to make a success of anything when your whole heart isn't in it, I don't know.'

'I shan't leave half of myself here. You're talking nonsense, Sarah—really.'

'No, I'm not. There are those women who can't see when they're lucky, and you're one of them. You have a good man, and good men are hard to come by. If you haven't the sense to see that then there are those who will. I think you get my meaning?'

'You mean Nancy?'

'I'm not mentioning names, but Pete is a full-blooded male, all man, and when things are offered to him on a plate, things he's having to do without while you're away—well, I don't have to spell it out.'

Rachelle moved uncomfortably. 'You have to have more than love, Sarah, to make a go of things. One grows tired of just giving and losing one's identity in someone else's. Sometimes it's like digging up a tree and replanting it somewhere else and it dies.'

Sarah put down the cream. 'Just according to who does the digging and replanting. If it's done with love then the tree survives. It might be a struggle at first, but it usually wins through.'

Rachelle smiled fondly at the pleasant face plump with a healthy colour.

'You'd make a good marriage counsellor, Sarah. Can I help you to do anything?'

'You go along in, everything is under control. You'll just have time to have a drink before I follow you.'

The meal was enjoyable, but Rachelle hardly touched a thing. She was polite and attentive all through dinner and Betty was unfailingly sweet to her. Geoff talked enthusiastically about the ranch and Pete was tolerantly amused by his enthusiasm.

Boyishly, he said, 'I wish you were coming back with us, Pete. There's such a lot I have to learn and you've been brought up in ranching.'

It was Minnie who answered. 'I never thought I would have a son who would end up on a ranch! All this enthusiasm could end in a damp squib. Pete left and you might too,' she said dryly.

Pete looked quizzically from one to the other. 'Whatever Geoff does in the future a spot of ranching will do him no harm. I can understand Minnie being sceptical. After all, it's a far different way of life from the U.K. We all have to find our own feet, cut our losses if they don't fit.'

Rachelle felt a little sick, feeling a jab in her direction from Pete's remark, and there was something else besides, the thought of leaving Pete with Nancy. Pete glanced at her with a hint of malice and she thought bleakly that this time next week she would not be here.

The evening went on its way with Pete and Geoff smoking cigars and talking about ranching while Rachelle, Minnie and Betty discussed recipes. Pete stayed talking to Geoff and helped him to make up his bed on the veranda after the women had gone to their rooms.

Rachelle undressed and slid into bed mechanically. Tomorrow Geoff, Betty and her mother would be gone. Then it would be her turn to leave. She would miss her mother; she was always so bright and talkative. But they would meet again—not like herself and Pete. His name was on her lips when the bedroom door opened and he came into the room.

'Are you asleep?' he whispered, closing the door. 'I'm switching on the light.'

Rachelle pushed herself up in bed, her heart threatening to knock a hole in her ribs. Pete was wearing a robe over his pyjama trousers, his hair was rumpled and fell across his forehead. He looked so boyish, so young that Rachelle hid emotions both quivering and exposed.

'What is it?' she asked, feeling herself go tight and closed again.

His eyes were twin points of light as he halted near the bed, and her eyes were riveted on the hirsute chest showing between the partly opened robe.

'I have a feeling that Betty might pop in before she goes to sleep. Move up,' he said.

Rachelle stiffened and drew up the bed cover to her throat.

'Don't worry,' he said sardonically. 'I only want you to move to one side of the bed so I can place another pillow beside you.'

Feeling foolish and not believing a word he said, Rachelle complied with an ill grace. As he leaned over her she felt his nearness unbearable. His male fragrance, the longing to feel his arms around her, the hard pressure of his lips on hers was almost too much.

'You can relax now,' he jeered, and bowed with mock gravity.

Rachelle felt scorching tears of anger and self-pity behind her eyes. Did he think her so naïve?

'Get out!' she cried. 'What do you ...'

His hand shot out and he was sitting down on the bed covering her mouth.

'Be quiet,' he whispered. 'I can hear voices in the corridor.'

He stood up at the tap on the door and went to open it.

'Hello, Betty. Come in.' Pete put his arm around his sister and closed the door behind her. 'Haven't changed, have you?'

Betty laughed up at him adoringly, then looked at Rachelle in bed.

'Did Pete tell you?' she asked, laughing. 'I always went to his room when I was small to say a special goodbye when he was going away to the city to school or leaving later for university.' She looked small against Pete's rangy height in her bare feet and dressing gown, but very happy. 'I can't believe Geoff is going home with me. I did hope you would come too, Pete, with Rachelle. The parents will adore her.'

'Some other time,' Pete murmured.

Betty put an arm around him. 'I want to thank you both for giving me Geoff—Rachelle because he's her brother and you, Pete, for being in this part of the world at the right time. If Rachelle had not been here I'm sure Geoff would have gone his way and forgotten all about me after writing one or two letters. Now we're going to be together for always.'

Rachelle said huskily, 'I'm very happy for you, Betty. There's no one I'd like better for a sister.'

'That goes for me too. There was another reason I came to speak to you now,' Betty looked up at her brother. 'Geoff wants you to know that he would never try to take your place at the ranch. He wants to work for a place of his own.'

Rachelle felt that some kind of remark was required from her at this point since Pete made no answer. The atmosphere of the room seemed to be filled with all the things she might have said. But what was the good of expanding on what Betty had said? The girl had only stated something she felt Pete should know; it would not be right for her to remark upon it. Nevertheless Rachelle was filled with a strange bitterness.

She said bleakly, 'You don't mind Mother going

with you? She isn't as scatty as she appears to be. She'll love you in time.'

Betty came forward to kiss her warmly. 'I love her already. I'll take good care of her.'

Rachelle saw her go in a mist of tears. A sob came unawares in her throat and made itself heard. Pete was there instantly. Bending over her, he pushed her down gently into bed and her heart jerked her into breathlessness as he tucked her up.

The sternness of his expression relaxed as he kissed her lips lightly. Softly, derisively, he whispered, 'I'm surprised at you crying for your mother. At your age too!'

When Pete had left the room Rachelle faced the agonising truth. She had to get away soon before she disgraced herself by telling her husband that she did not want to leave him.

It was a bright clear day with white clouds sailing across the blue sky, and Rachelle knew she would be glad when Geoff, Betty and her mother had gone— one of the last acts in a series of disturbing moves nearing the last final curtain.

Rachelle awoke with the feeling that the day would be more difficult to get through when she was on her own with Pete. Minnie came in to see her, all bright and chirpy.

'I feel quite excited about going with Geoff,' she said. 'I suppose you're determined to go back and carry on with your career?' She moved to the dressing table to pick up a cut glass scent spray and sniff it with appreciation. 'How long do you intend to stay with Pete?' she added warily.

Rachelle ran the comb through her hair and wished she did not look so heavy-eyed. Her reflection in the mirror stared back at her unhappily and she squared slim shoulders.

'No longer than is necessary. I want to go back in order to get settled,' she replied dully.

Minnie cast her a careful glance. 'You don't sound very enthusiastic about it,' she remarked frankly. 'It isn't too late to come with us. Pete could follow later. We could go back home together. If Dad does get married again I might sell the house and ask Tony Spelling for a flat near to you.'

Rachelle patted the bright hair and ran the tip of a finger over her shapely eyebrows.

'You must do as you wish, Mother. I must say how happy I am that you're accepting Betty as Geoff's wife. I'm sure they're going to be very happy.'

Minnie shrugged as she put down the scent spray. 'Nothing I could do about it, since Geoff was so determined. Mind you, I had no chance to get him to change his mind with Betty there all the time. It was a clever move on her part to take him out to talk things over.'

Rachelle said helplessly, 'But, Mother, Betty is in love and she's fighting for her man. You would have done the same.'

Minnie sighed. 'Pity you don't begin fighting for yours instead of going in for a career. You could get Pete back if you wanted.'

'I don't want to talk about it.'

Pete had gone out when they went in to breakfast, but he was soon back with a cablegram which he tossed on the table to Minnie before the meal was over.

'This has just come. I hope it isn't bad news,' he said gravely.

Minnie changed colour. 'You open.it, Pete. I just haven't the courage.'

Pete slit the envelope open and scanned the contents.

His teeth were a bar of whiteness in his tanned face as he lifted his head.

'Great news!' he exclaimed. 'Sam was married yesterday to Mrs Carne, and they're moving in to her bungalow.'

He tossed the paper to Minnie and met Rachelle's eyes with mockery in his as if to say, What did I tell you? Tears rushed to her eyes as it occurred to her that but for Pete's intervention her grandpa might now be languishing in an old folks' home. She was too choked for words, but she did manage to hold his gaze and say, 'Thank you for helping Grandpa.'

Minnie added her thanks as well and looked a little stunned. The meal ended on a bright note and it was a happy send-off. There were kisses and promises to meet again soon. Then Pete was standing with his arm loosely around Rachelle's shoulders as the car slid away to disappear in the dust of a beautiful morning.

Immediately the car had gone Pete dropped his arm from her shoulders.

'Would you send a cable back for us all?' she asked, looking no higher than his lean tanned jaw. 'Tell Grandpa how delighted we all are, and that I shall be seeing him soon.'

'Delighted to,' he answered.

His hand fell on her arm as she would have walked into the bungalow.

'You didn't make much of a breakfast again this morning, I noticed. I hope you do better at lunch or I'm sending for the doctor,' he said. 'There's something wrong when a girl like you goes off her food.'

'There's nothing wrong with me,' she cried, on the defensive. 'And let go of my arm, you're hurting. I have problems and I'll eat when I'm hungry.'

'I have problems too, or haven't you noticed?' His eyes were glittering, his teeth closed and tight with anger. 'I have the sense to eat my food. It's for your good and mine that you behave normally and not like some lovesick schoolgirl. Who is it you're pining for, Jake or Tony Spelling?'

Rachelle tightened up inside. He meant to hurt, but she was determined that he would not see how much he had succeeded.

'I've had enough with one man without taking on anyone else,' she retorted. 'And please leave me alone. What I do or eat is my own affair.'

'It's mine as well. I don't have to deal with a sick wife on top of my other problems, and I'm going to see that it does not happen.'

Rachelle shook her arm free of his grasp. 'You're the last person I would want to look after me if I was ill. Don't worry, I shan't be a burden to you much longer. I can pack now if you like.'

'You'll go when I let you go and not before. Try any hanky-panky and you know what to expect. Is that understood?'

Rachelle gave him one smouldering look and went indoors. Wallowing in deep depression, she went to her room and gave her mind to writing a letter to her grandfather. At least that was a ray of sunshine, along with Geoff's engagement to Betty. Her grandfather would be delighted to hear the news. He had long said that it was time Geoff settled down.

She went to the kitchen to have a coffee with Sarah

around mid-morning and gave her the letter to post, together with Pete's other mail. Sarah was tickled pink to hear about Grandpa and as she prepared the lunch later Rachelle washed the dishes she used. Pete did not come in to lunch. Jake came at midday to collect it. While Sarah packed it he talked to Rachelle, who was eating in the kitchen.

His eyes roved over her bright hair and delicate complexion with approval.

'You look good enough to eat,' he drawled.

Sarah chimed in, 'Said the big bad wolf! You leave Rachelle alone. She has all the compliments she needs from her husband.'

Jake eyed Sarah boldly. 'Every woman likes compliments from a man. Has anyone ever told you you're sweet?'

Sarah blushed. 'Get on with you! Flattery will get you nowhere.'

She gave him the lunch box and his look included them both.

'Nancy didn't turn up for work this morning. Too tight, I'd say,' he commented dryly. 'So long. Be seeing you.'

When he had gone, Rachelle asked, 'Does Nancy drink a lot?'

'Sometimes,' Sarah replied. 'This is no place for a single woman. Pete has had a steadying influence on her, but she does go off the rails from time to time.'

'Do you think I'd better pay her a call?'

'Wouldn't do any good. Pete's the only one, like I said, who has any influence with her.'

The afternoon passed all too swiftly, perhaps because Rachelle was dreading the evening with Pete. She washed her lingerie, shampooed her hair and pressed her dress for that evening. Dressing for dinner lifted her morale. She heard Pete go into his room and there were sounds which told her that he was taking a shower and changing.

She was ready on time in a long-sleeved, high-waisted dress which made her feel elegant. Full-skirted, its neckline plunged demurely to show the hint of the dividing line at her breast. It was slightly daring for Rachelle's conservative taste in dress, but she had to admit pleasure at her reflection in the mirror.

With trembling hands she smoothed down the lovely chiffon skirt in a flattering shade of amber, added gold studs to her ears with a matching chain necklace and padlocked a bracelet to her slender wrist. When Pete tapped on her door her heart began to beat in thick slow thumps. He wore a dark suit and white shirt against which he looked tanned and very fit.

He looked so attractive, so dear, that Rachelle had to lower her eyes quickly before he read in them the longing for his nearness. But not before she had seen him taking in her whole appearance before meeting her eyes.

He gave a low whistle of appreciation. 'One thing I like about you is that you're always ready on time and you always look perfect.'

The dinner was not the ordeal she had expected. Pete treated it in the way of a celebration for Sam's wedding. He uncorked a bottle of champagne and filled her glass.

'You'd better eat a good dinner this evening since we're drinking this bottle of champagne between us, and we all know how lethal alcohol is on an empty stomach,' he said darkly.

'Point made,' she answered, raising her glass to her lips.

'I haven't finished yet,' he went on with a wicked twinkle in his eye. 'It's imperative that you keep sober since I'm celebrating too, and you know what that can mean. I don't mean to frighten you, but I must warn you.'

'That's blackmail!' she retorted, and lifted her glass. 'Here's to Grandpa. A long and very happy marriage.'

Pete seconded the toast and raised an expressive eyebrow.

'Don't look at me like that,' he warned, 'or I might feel inclined to retaliate!'

Rachelle looked at him dazedly, her heart was thumping so hard she was sure he could hear it.

'How am I looking?' she asked with a tremor. Heaven forbid that her love for him had been expressed in her face. Not that, she thought, I couldn't bear it if he knew that I loved him when he has no love for me.

He gave an ironical smile. 'You're tempting me,' he confessed with a drawl. 'You sit there en déshabille and dewy-eyed and expect me to remain unmoved. You and I must have a talk after dinner. This can't go on—you know that as well as I do. However, Sarah has excelled herself in preparing a special meal just for the two of us. See that you eat your share in appreciation.'

He went on to say that he had sent a wire to Sam congratulating him and repeating his invitation to come with his wife to spend a holiday with him. Rachelle, listening to his deep disturbing voice, told herself that if her marriage had failed where she was concerned at least it had brought nothing but good and possibly lasting happiness to her beloved Grandpa.

Minnie also had benefited. She had been teetering on the brink of uncertainty regarding the house and her father, and this trip out away from all her problems would do her a world of good.

'I'm very grateful,' Rachelle told him, 'for what you've done towards settling Grandpa and bringing Mother out of her lethargy over her problems. I appreciate it, Pete.'

Pete gave a short unpleasant laugh. 'What have you been doing, my sweet? Dissecting our marriage and pinpointing the good things emerging from it. That's one way of looking at it.'

The colour crept beneath her clear skin and she dabbed her mouth with the table napkin. She said stiffly,

'You needn't be so off-hand about it. I was only telling you how I appreciate what you've done for the two people I love. There's Geoff as well. You don't know how happy it's made me to know that he's going to settle down with a girl who will make him a wonderful wife.'

His mouth thinned. 'Nice to know that you're happy for once, but spare me the gratitude.' There was a growing hostility in his eyes, his manner. 'I like your family.'

Rachelle swallowed on a lump in her throat at the obvious implication that he did not like her, his wife. Sarah came in with a special dessert that she knew was Pete's favourite dish and Rachelle tried to behave normally by giving her a warm smile. If she had needed further confirmation that her marriage was over here it was.

Every spoonful of the delicious cheesecake she put into her mouth threatened to choke her. There was a sharp brittle silence during which Rachelle felt the emotion of shedding tears inwardly. There was a wall in between them that even she, Pete's wife, found insurmountable.

From somewhere came the courage for her to hold out the olive branch. 'I'm sorry, Pete ...'

The sound of brakes shrieking followed by the dull thud of impact shook the bungalow, leaving Rachelle staring at Pete with horror. He was on his feet immediately and she found herself alone, too shaken to do anything. Then Sarah came in, agitated and shaking.

'I always said this would happen,' she cried. 'That car is much too powerful for Nancy to handle. I've seen it coming, but she wouldn't listen.'

'What are you talking about?' Rachelle demanded. 'Sit down, Sarah, and compose yourself.'

Rachelle thought this was ironical coming from someone like herself since she was trembling in every limb herself, fearing the worst. She patted the hand Sarah put on the table as she sat down in the chair Pete had vacated, and waited for her to pull herself together.

'She was there scorching along and missing the entrance to the bungalow,' she said at last. 'I saw her from the kitchen window. It seemed she changed her mind about driving past and decided to call at the last moment.'

'You mean Nancy?'

Sarah nodded. 'She swerved suddenly in at the entrance gate, lost control and smashed the car into a tree.'

Rachelle lost colour, then she too was on her feet and running to the veranda. A shudder ran through her at the sight of the big car jammed against a tree. Thank heaven it had not caught fire, was her first thought.

Seconds later she was blessing the fact that the car had not hit the tree head-on. The right wheel had taken most of the impact. Pete was bending inside the car, the whiteness of his shirt showing up in the cuffs and front in the half light. Slowly he was lifting Nancy from the driving seat. The red hair flowed over his arm as he drew her towards him, then he was striding towards Rachelle bearing the unconscious Nancy in his arms.

As he came nearer Rachelle saw the wound on Nancy's forehead slowly covering her face with blood. She shuddered, beyond words, and stared with horror. 'Is she badly hurt?' she whispered through pale lips. 'I don't think so,' he replied. 'Where's Sarah?'

By the time Rachelle had boiled the kettle of water, filled a bowl and collected towels along with the first aid box, Sarah had stripped Nancy of her clothes, put her in a nightdress and covered her up in bed.

Sarah had put her in the room Betty, Pete's sister, had occupied, and Rachelle watched while Sarah bathed the unconscious face to the smell of antiseptic.

'At least her face isn't damaged,' Rachelle said shakily. 'Is she badly hurt?'

'Pete doesn't think so. He's gone all over her body and everything appears to be unbroken, but he's leaving nothing to chance. That's why he's gone for the doctor himself, to make sure he comes back with him.'

Rachelle said, 'Is there anything I can do, Sarah?'

'Not much yet. I'm sure Nancy will be very grateful for your loan of a nightie. I hope she isn't too badly concussed. This wound on her forehead is more of a bruise, even though it's bled profusely.'

Nancy had come round when Pete returned with the doctor in the small hours. He was a retired surgeon

who came out in any emergency. Rachelle went into
the lounge when he went in to see Nancy with Pete.
She had made coffee when Pete joined her after the
surgeon had gone.

'What does he say?' she asked, giving him a cup of
steaming liquid.

'Slight concussion, but no other injuries as far as he
can see. He suggests that she rests for several days and
if there are any aches or pains we're to contact him
immediately. You should be in bed,' he added curtly.

She watched him finish the coffee. To her caring
eyes he looked tired and fed up. She daren't guess at
the speed he had put on in the car in search of a doctor.
He would not spare himself. Did Nancy mean that
much to him? If his ravaged looks were anything to
go by, she did.

'So should you,' she answered.

He set the cup down on the tray, said carelessly, 'I'm
sitting up with Nancy tonight in case she lapses into
unconsciousness. You never can tell with concussion.'

She said eagerly, 'Let me help. I can sit with Nancy
while you have a rest.'

Curtly, he said, 'I can cope. Go to bed.'

'But ...'

'I said go to bed.'

Rachelle put down her cup and rose to her feet.
Without another look in his direction she went to the
door.

'Thanks for what you've done for Nancy,' said Pete.

Rachelle did not pause or turn. She left the room
blindly, knowing that she would have changed places
with Nancy gladly. But it was futile to wish she could
be once more with Pete. She had lost him, and it was
her own fault.

CHAPTER NINE

RACHELLE awoke around ten o'clock with a heavy head. Her first waking thought was for Pete and Nancy and, feeling guilty for oversleeping, she washed and dressed hurriedly. Sarah looked up in surprise when she walked into the kitchen.

'Up already?' she said with a smile. 'Pete was hoping you'd sleep until lunch time.' Her perusal of the pale face and shadowed eyes was kind. 'You don't look as if you slept well. Bad head?'

Rachelle gave a pale smile. 'A bit heavy. How is Nancy this morning?'

Sarah went briskly to one of the kitchen cupboards and came back with something in a cup which she gave to Rachelle as she sat down at the kitchen table.

'Drink this, it will clear your head. Nancy is fine and Pete has gone to work. Now let's see you eat some breakfast.'

Rachelle did her best, but every mouthful seemed to stick in her throat. By the time she had finished eating, several people had called to enquire about Nancy. Jake and Bill popped in, but Sarah refused to let them see her, saying that the girl had to be kept quiet and rest.

Around mid-morning Rachelle went in to see Nancy with a drink and the matching negligé to the nightdress she had lent her. The red hair was strewn all over the pillow, the tawny lashes resting on pale fatigued cheeks. The dressing on her forehead gave her a vulnerable look and Rachelle was relieved to see her open her eyes.

Rachelle gave her a warm smile. 'How are you feeling? Better, I hope?'

Nancy stretched luxuriously. 'My head is a bit muzzy, but otherwise I feel fine. Where's Pete?'

'He's gone to work. Let me help you on with this, then you can sit up to have your drink.'

She put down the tray and took the negligé from her arm. It was an exquisite thing of frothy elegance, matching the pale turquoise nightdress Nancy was wearing.

'Very nice,' Nancy murmured, pushing herself up in the bed and putting her arms behind her for Rachelle to put on the negligé. 'Goes with my hair, don't you think?'

Rachelle agreed. 'When you've had your drink I'll fetch a bowl of water for you to sponge your hands and face.'

Nancy patted the ribbon and lace in place. Smugly she said,

'It won't be necessary. Pete has seen to that before he left this morning. Wasn't it sweet of him to sit up with me? We're very close, you know.'

The tawny eyes gleamed between thick lashes to see how Rachelle was taking it. Rachelle, for her part, felt every word like a sting from a scorpion, but she managed a smile.

She said dryly, 'Pete is very gallant. You were lucky to escape with minor injuries.'

'I was, wasn't I?' Nancy took the drink and eyed Rachelle over the top. 'But then Pete has been lucky for me all along. I don't know what I would have done

without him when Daddy died. I wanted to die too.
Only Pete understood how I felt.'

Rachelle gazed at the tears on the tawny lashes and
wondered if they were genuine, then upbraided herself
for such unworthy thoughts.

She said quietly, 'That's a big powerful car you
have. Wouldn't you be better with something smaller?'

Nancy lifted her chin. 'I'm quite capable of handling it,' she retorted huffily. 'Besides, I might have been
hurt far more if the car hood hadn't been as long as
it is.'

Rachelle sank down on to the side of the bed. The
negligé she had loaned Nancy enhanced her colouring
and she looked vulnerable, very pretty despite the
dressing on her forehead and the shadows beneath the
amber eyes. Had she deliberately smashed the car into
the tree? It could not have been more successful if she
had. If she had not then she was the darling of fate.

Rachelle made an effort to sort out her confused
thoughts, reviewing with candid speculation Nancy's
attempts, if any, to break up her marriage. Pete had
always been tolerant in regard to women. He had
always been protective and kind. His sympathetic
compassion for Nancy when she had lost her father was
not wrongly placed, Rachelle conceded. On the other
hand, it was a very strong weapon for Nancy to use in
bringing him to heel.

She trembled with apprehension but refused to
panic. If Nancy pushed her too far she would tell Pete
that she did not want to leave him, tell him of her love
for him. It would mean irrevocable surrender, the
throwing away of a career she had long set her heart
on. It would also leave her vulnerable to hurt. Shiver-
ing a little, Rachelle dragged herself back to the present.

Nancy was saying, 'Now my car is out of action I shall have to rely upon Pete to give me the occasional lift. But I'm sure he won't mind.'

Her voice was as smooth as cream, but Rachelle refused to be provoked. Gradually regaining her composure, she smiled sweetly. 'I'm sure Pete will only be too happy to oblige until he finds you a replacement while your car is off the road,' she answered without rancour.

The amber eyes glinted as Nancy finished her drink and put the cup down on the tray beside her bed.

'That's an idea,' she said, well pleased with the way things were going. 'Pete could take me to choose one, have the day out together.'

Rachelle laughed. 'You won't get Pete away from his job that easily. By the way, how is it going? Pete never talks about his job to me since he knows I don't understand it. It's a painful subject to me anyway.'

Long lashes veiled the tawny eyes. 'I don't hold out much hope that a strike will make our fortunes. We have to cover the costs of the drilling, which are considerable. But we enjoy the challenge, Pete and I. Mind you, it was a hunch of my father's that there is oil in these parts, and his hunches in the past more or less paid off. But he isn't here now, is he? Worried about your shares, are you?'

Rachelle stiffened. The claws were out again, she thought.

'That was a rotten thing to say!' she retorted. 'But I refuse to get angry with you, since you aren't well.'

'If I were you,' Nancy murmured silkily, 'I'd get rid of those shares you hold in the company while you can still make a profit. I'll give you whatever price you ask for them.'

'But isn't that bad business on your part?' Rachelle

taunted softly. 'Come to think of it, Jake suggested I sell my shares to him. Of course I know why he wants them. He wants to hold more shares than Pete to give him the upper hand in the company. Is that why you want them, Nancy, to bring Pete to heel?'

Nancy flushed angrily, 'How dare you accuse me of double dealing? Wait until I tell Pete!' she blustered.

'Will you tell Pete? I doubt it.' Rachelle rose to her feet, sickened by the whole thing. She had been right to get out of it.

Nancy watched her go with a smouldering look of hate, but Rachelle ignored it. Suddenly her head was throbbing terribly. All was quiet when she went outdoors to lift her face to the sparkling air. All the light had gone from her face now since the bold front to convince Nancy was no longer necessary, and it was small and pinched-looking.

There was a slight mist over the land. There were occasional glimpses of the distant hills, solid and reassuring. Dark hollows screened by gorse, low, wind-twisted trees in grotesque shapes, then the creek dreaming in a thinly veiled haze—the scene before her now was familiar and heart-warming.

Rachelle sat by the creek until the mist lifted and the sun came out. Drawing up her knees, she hugged them with her arms and lowered her forehead on them. The sun had come out, but not on her world. Was she destined to go through life in search of peace and happiness? Was the right way to go on or go back to a man who could no longer want her? She felt an unexpected surge of mutiny. Nancy taking her place—the thought of it sent the colour rising in her face, only to fade again in a wave of coldness which seemed to touch her heart. There was the sickening feeling of having walked into a trap. An appalling sense of doom enfolded her like a cloak. It was a long time before she was able to compel herself to calmness.

Pete was on the veranda steps when he saw her returning to the bungalow. He waited until she joined him. Her face had the luminous pearly glow of the white drifting clouds above them and he narrowed his gaze as she avoided his eyes, retreating a little.

'You haven't much colour,' he said. 'Sarah says you didn't eat much breakfast.'

Rachelle felt a hardness masking her face eating into her at the thought that he had called while she was out to see Nancy.

'Don't you think you should concentrate on one invalid at a time?' she said sarcastically. 'And mind your own business while you're doing just that.'

His dark intent face, controlled, expressionless, did not alter. His look cut her down to size.

'So you resent Nancy being here? There was no other choice. It was better for her not to be moved until the concussion was no longer a danger. You should have stayed in bed and had a good rest after being up all night.'

'Don't worry,' she replied caustically, 'I haven't forgotten what you said about having an invalid wife on your hands. Apparently an invalid mistress is a different proposition.'

His eyes glittered dangerously. His self-restraint was admirable. He spoke quietly.

'If you're trying to pick a quarrel with me you're wasting your time and mine. I refuse to quarrel with you. Have a rest after lunch, it will help your frayed nerves. Nancy won't be here long.'

Neither shall I, Rachelle told herself inwardly. 'I won't get in your way,' she answered. 'Incidentally,

you can have those shares of mine in the company. I
think it's better to break all ties, don't you?'

Pete said angrily, 'I don't know what's got into you.
If Nancy has said anything to bring this mood on I can
deal with it.'

'Oh, sure. You can deal with anything.' White-faced,
hands clenched, Rachelle blazed up at him. 'Why
don't you go out there and order those clever drills of
yours to come up with some positive results?'

He had his hand on her arm as she would have
passed him indoors when one of the men came running
up from the field, a flaxen-haired young man called
Snowy. He acknowledged Rachelle quickly with a brief
salute before turning to Pete to speak in an undertone.
Pete dropped down the steps of the veranda and was
away with him, leaving Rachelle to drag herself indoors.

Useless to tell herself that she was the one who had
a right to be angry. She was a fool to match her wits
with a man of his experience. Despair was something
she was beginning to know only too well.

Pete did not come in for lunch; Sarah said there was
a problem with the drilling. She was alarmed at the
small amount Rachelle ate for lunch and packed her off
to bed with another painkiller, telling her that the
draught would work if she relaxed and rested. Rachelle slept for most of the afternoon and awoke feeling
refreshed.

She gave herself no time to think of meeting Pete
again as she washed and dressed for the evening meal.
Not that she had any appetite. There were angry
sounds coming from Nancy's room as she opened her
door, and the next moment Jake came out and nearly
knocked her down in his hurry to be gone. He mut-

tered something in the way of an apology and was gone.

'What's going on?' she asked Sarah in the kitchen.

'Heaven knows!' Sarah straightened from the cooker to close the door on savoury smells, and turned a face flushed from the heat. 'Goodness, I shall be glad when Nancy's gone home! I knew she'd bring trouble. Jake went in to see her with flowers from the men. The next thing is they're quarrelling and Jake comes out as sore as a bear disturbed eating honey. Good thing Pete wasn't in, he would have had Jake out in no time. As it is Pete's going to be late in this evening, so he wants you to eat without him. Nancy is getting up, so you'll have company. And for goodness' sake eat something or I shall begin to wonder what I'm doing here at all!'

Rachelle kissed her flushed cheek. 'You're a darling, Sarah, and you know you'll never leave Pete. I don't know why you're always so nice to me. That second dose did the trick,' she added. 'I feel fine after the rest. Thanks a lot.'

Sarah said shortly, 'You can show your thanks by eating something for a change. At least I can load some of my cooking on Nancy.'

Nancy was very disappointed that Pete did not join them and sulked mostly through the meal. Pete came in when they were at the coffee stage. His deep voice, in teasing mood, was heard coming from the kitchen where he was talking to Sarah. Then all was quiet as he went to take a shower.

He has all the women going gooey-eyed over him, thought Rachelle. Nancy perked up on hearing him and pooh-poohed Sarah's suggestion that she should go back to bed again and have an early night. Rachelle, however, was not in the mood to see him with Nancy, so she went quietly to her room. She was in the kitchen when Pete went into the lounge, helping with the dishes before going to her room.

Rachelle had tried to sleep, but the thought of Pete with Nancy was more than she could bear. But being alone with her torment was preferable to seeing Nancy's triumphant glances.

Tossing and turning, she told herself that anything was better than torturous thoughts. She was still awake when the tap came on her door. Rachelle quelled the racing of her heart and lay quivering. The tap came again, this time more peremptory, and Pete said her name. Her first reaction was to let him go on knocking because she had locked the door, but he knew she was a light sleeper.

Slipping on her wrap, she opened the door and her hand moved to the light switch. Pete entered and closed the door behind him. In her bare feet with the silk wrap showing tender curves, and her hair tousled, Rachelle looked like a child awakened from sleep.

But there was no tender appraisal from Pete. He towered above her, wide-shouldered and narrow-eyed. The room, flooded with light, enhanced his clean-cut features, the fine intelligent grey eyes and firmly modelled mouth. It made Rachelle feel weak just to look at him. She wanted him so much—but he was in no mood for the talk of lovers.

He said with heavy satire, 'Thanks for waiting up for me. One can hardly call nine o'clock the middle of the night.'

'But it's late now,' she answered on the defensive. 'I hope Nancy filled in for me. I'm sure she did it very well.'

He said grimly, 'I've had a hard day, and I'm in no mood for sarcasm, least of all from you.'

'But it's all right if it comes from you,' she flashed.

He made to turn away, paused and shoved his hands into his pockets.

'Nancy waited for me in spite of feeling tired. How do you expect me to feel when you couldn't have cared less?'

'Oh, sure,' Rachelle blazed. 'Perhaps Nancy had good reason to wait for you. She must have had good reason for lying. Sarah wanted her to go to bed after we'd eaten, but Nancy insisted on staying put. She wasn't in the least tired. She's got you just where she wants you.'

'And where may that be?' Pete demanded in tones of steel.

Rachelle was trembling. She said unsteadily, 'You know—why ask me?'

'I don't know. What I do know is that you're jealous of Nancy.'

'That's nothing to do with it. I'm hardly likely to welcome you from her arms.'

There was a hint of malice in his smile. 'So that's what you think,' he said softly. 'If I'd left her arms it wouldn't be to come to yours, since we're hardly on speaking terms. Are we?'

Rachelle shrugged and turned away. He caught her by the shoulder and swung her round.

'I said, are we?' he repeated.

She lifted her eyes to his dark face. 'Good thing we aren't! I'd hate to think that after kissing Nancy you came ...'

'To you?' he finished for her. His eyes narrowed cruelly and he drew her slowly in his arms. 'Seeing that you object to Nancy's kisses on my lips what about erasing them?'

He forced her mouth to the will of his own. It was like teetering on the brink of a furnace. The heat took her breath away as she clung. The punishing kiss was one that raging insistence lengthened until Rachelle sagged in his arms before he let her go.

'You asked for that,' he said thickly. 'But that's as far as it goes. I wish to heaven I'd never seen you!'

As the door closed behind him Rachelle covered her burning face with her hands. She was trembling from head to foot, her bruised mouth was quivering, and she wished she was dead. Stumbling to the bed, she crept in between the sheets and lay staring up at the ceiling. It was a long time before she turned on to her side and let the tears come.

Two days went by and on the morning of the second day, Pete had brought a car for Nancy to use until her own was repaired. Sarah had called Rachelle to look through the kitchen window to the scene outside. Pete, clad in working gear, was showing Nancy over a dark blue car. It was smaller than her own and more compact. Nancy was smiling up at him, evidently pleased, and as he playfully ruffled her hair, she reached up to kiss him. Then they both got into the car, Nancy driving, presumably to try it out.

Rachelle stood at the window staring after them. All feeling seemed to have left her. The inner conflict of the last two days had wrung her dry of any emotion. There had been times when she had been on the brink of packing her bags and leaving. It was only out of consideration for Pete that she had stayed.

Leaving Nancy under the same roof as her husband

would have caused gossip, so for the short time Nancy was there Rachelle gritted her teeth and decided to stick it out. She had filled in most of her time by doing household chores, cleaning out cupboards and spring-cleaning the rooms. Nancy was allowed visitors now and most of the staff on the workings had been in to see her.

Hearing them laughing and talking as she went about her chores, Rachelle conceded that while Nancy left a lot to be desired in the way of flaunting her charms, she was a kind of highlight in a small community where nothing happened to relieve the monotony. As for Pete, he had been out most of the last two days and Nancy had dined with them in the evening, which had cut the necessity of a prolonged conversation between them.

Now time was running out. That evening there was to be a special little dinner for Nancy's recovery, and Rachelle was helping Sarah with the cooking.

Rachelle turned round from the kitchen window as Sarah spoke.

'I can't wait to see that girl on her way,' she remarked, standing up to her elbows in flour at the kitchen table. 'Pete hasn't been the same since she came. I've never known him to be so short-tempered. He's always been so easy-going, and here's you drifting around like something from *Macbeth*!'

Rachelle laughed as she proceeded to toss a salad for lunch.

'I'm sorry, Sarah. The after-effects of the accident, I suppose. Let's be thankful that it was no worse.'

'I'm not so sure about that, and I'm not exactly thinking of the accident,' Sarah retorted darkly. 'That girl is up to something, you mark my words.'

Rachelle did not answer. She was seeing Pete as he had been these last few days, his dark hair rough and tousled, his mouth set and weary in the bronze of his face. There were problems with the drilling and he was out all day. It was wrong for him to work so hard, to worry himself silly on a project which had all the signs of being a failure. His was the face of a man who had nothing but his own strength to hold on to in a bitter struggle against the odds.

Rachelle had watched him covertly, then tenderly, for in spite of his tall wide-shouldered figure, his virile masculinity, he had looked so boyish, so dear in his unawareness of her scrutiny, that her heart swelled with love for him. I have to help him, comfort him, she thought, and what better way than to tell him the truth, that I love him? I know he said he wished we'd never met, but he might not have meant it. Her thoughts whirled in a new golden dawn of happiness. Pete needs kindness from me, even if he does prefer Nancy. What an idiot I've been, to let unpleasant incidents change my whole personality! That's not the real me, that hard and scathing being who spits out because of hurt.

Without being aware of it Rachelle found herself humming softly as she tossed the salad. Sarah looked across the table in surprise, then lowered her eyes with a secret little smile.

Nancy came in for lunch full of praises for the car Pete had procured for her.

'It goes like a dream,' she said smugly. 'I might keep it as well as my other.'

Sarah just grunted and Rachelle said brightly, 'Who knows, you might grow really attached to it.'

Nancy wiggled her way from the room with a case containing a dress for that evening fetched from home along with other things she needed. She spent the afternoon washing her hair and preparing for the evening.

That afternoon Sarah slipped in the kitchen while making an afternoon drink and hurt her ankle. Instantly Rachelle had her on a chair and was bathing the ankle alternately in hot and cold water.

'Stop making a fuss,' Sarah protested. 'I haven't sprained it, I'm only shaken by the fall, that's all.'

Rachelle bound up the ankle despite her protest, gave her a hot sweet drink to treat the shock and helped her to her room.

'I'm not staying here,' Sarah told her. 'What about the dinner this evening?'

'I can take care of that,' Rachelle told her firmly. 'You're going to rest for a change.' The colour was coming back to Sarah's face and she looked more like her old self. Rachelle smiled. 'You're looking better already. I can cope. Don't you dare get up. I'll send Pete in with your meal.'

Rachelle washed and changed early that evening and called in to see Nancy on her way to the kitchen. She found her making up her face, fast on the road to recovery. The red hair was a flame of colour tied back with a ribbon as Nancy turned from the mirror to flutter eyelashes dark with mascara.

'Hello,' she said. 'You're early.'

Rachelle said, 'Sarah has hurt her ankle, so I shall be serving the dinner.'

'Sorry about that. I must buy her a present for looking after me,' Nancy added.

'Sarah won't expect anything,' Rachelle assured her. 'Like the rest of us she's only too glad to help. We're all thankful your accident wasn't any worse.'

The tawny eyes glittered between the blackened lashes as they glided over Rachelle's slender enchanting figure in the square-necked silk dress with its little lace jacket. She noted the lightly made up eyes, the clear skin, and the sweetness of her expression, and her own expression became soured.

'I'm sure you are,' she said. 'I know Pete is.'

Rachelle smiled. 'That's why he's insisted that only the three of us should celebrate your recovery. He doesn't want you to overdo things,' she said quietly.

A strange light came into the tawny eyes. Nancy said softly,

'Pete is so understanding. He knows that when the car crash happened I was feeling desperately unhappy. You were right about the new car he's bought for me. It's much better for me than the old one. I do hope you forgive me for being so horrid to you.'

Recoiling from the idea of Pete buying the car, Rachelle said offhandedly, 'There's nothing to forgive.'

'Ah, but there is.' Nancy's voice was as smooth as silk. 'It was only natural for Pete and me to get fond of each other while you were away. After all, we are two of a kind. That was why I wanted to buy your shares in the company. I wanted to give them to Pete for being so good to me.'

'Why not make him a present of your own shares? Not that he would accept them.'

The false smile broadened into a triumphant smirk. 'He will have them eventually, won't he? All I have will be his one day.'

Rachelle was deliberately obtuse. 'I fail to see your point, but I'll work on it. See you later.'

Rachelle went to the kitchen and tied an apron over her dress, wondering why she had bothered to go to

Nancy's room in the first place. A sense of duty had taken her there, and concern in case she was not as well as she appeared to be. The girl had suffered a slight concussion and Rachelle could not forget being angry with her on her first night under her roof.

However, her sympathy was misplaced since Nancy was as tough as old boots anyway. She was wondering what kind of dress the girl was wearing this evening—something to knock Pete's eyeballs out, she would bet. She was smiling when Pete arrived. There was a smear of oil on his right cheek and he looked jaded, which was alarming in Pete.

He grinned whitely, 'A picture of pure domestic bliss,' he drawled, leaning sideways against the door frame. 'Where's Sarah?'

'Taking a rest in her room. I'm serving the meal,' Rachelle answered, putting on oven gloves. 'You might look in on her when you go for a shower.'

He looked serious. 'Anything wrong?' he queried.

'No.'

Rachelle was lighting the candles on the dining table when Pete strolled in with Nancy on his arm. Nancy looked striking in a dress of green floating material swathed around her bust showing every line of her shapely curves. Her look at Rachelle said plainly that she had not a chance where Pete was concerned.

Rachelle took one last glance at the beautifully prepared table, tweaked a flower into place on the arrangement in the centre and addressed Pete.

'Will you take Sarah's dinner to her room while I bring the food in? It's ready.'

Pete handed round the champagne and when he gave Rachelle her glass their eyes met and held for seconds while she coloured like a rose.

Pete's eyes were openly mocking. 'Two lovely ladies to dine with me,' he drawled.

Rachelle was aware of him towering above her as she moved aside without a word. It was impossible to answer with Nancy's eyes intent upon her with their expression of pity, malice and curiosity. It was like being under a microscope, thought Rachelle, knowing her cheeks were dyed brilliantly with colour. The silky sheen of her brown hair, and the deep blue of her eyes, gave her a vivid loveliness of which she herself was unaware.

Disconcerted with Pete's eyes also upon her, Rachelle put a hand to her face, felt it burn like fire and lifted her glass.

'Here's to your complete recovery, Nancy. Cheers,' she said, feeling foolish.

The bubbling champagne tingled up her nose, making her blink. She had a desire to giggle. Lighthearted, she thought, I don't really care about Nancy and her presence here. I'm not afraid of her now—not since I made up my mind to make it up with Pete.

With a small amused smile that was enchanting, Rachelle lifted her glass again.

'Here's to my darling husband and his venture in oil. May it be successful soon.'

She drank again from her glass and giggled at the expression on Nancy's face. She was utterly dumbfounded, but Pete was not amused. His dark face hardened a little, his tones were sardonic.

'Thanks. Most encouraging.' The grey eyes narrowed and he lifted a provocative brow. 'Do I return the compliment and wish you success in yours?'

Nancy murmured, 'To your new venture, Rachelle.' The amber eyes glinted as she turned to Pete after sipping her drink. 'Rachelle is concerned about you, Pete,' she added. 'She's been asking me what are our chances of striking oil. After all, if we do strike oil Rachelle won't have to bother about a career, will she?'

A cold feeling clutched Rachelle's heart, closing around it with a choking sensation. She was uncertain now just how much Pete and Nancy shared the interests of the company. Were they hand in glove? Did Pete really love Nancy? There was only one way to find out—to confront Pete later that evening when Nancy had gone to her room.

Pete had not said a word. He had finished his drink and seated Nancy at the table. Hardly knowing what she was doing, Rachelle proceeded to hand around the hot plates.

'I'll do that,' Pete said curtly. 'Sit down.'

Rachelle was about to protest as he pulled out her chair at the table, but before she could say a word they were alerted by sounds and a sudden roar. Immediately Pete was out on the veranda, looking towards the oil-fields where a pall of darkness seemed to be hanging in the sky. The air stank with it. Oil!

'We've done it!' cried Pete. 'We've struck oil! Yippee!'

Nancy and Rachelle had joined him and he caught Nancy, who was nearest, in his arms and lifted her in the air. She put her arms around his neck and neither of them saw Rachelle go back into the house.

Pete and Nancy had gone to join the men, who were watching the oil gushing up into the fading night sky. Jake came running with a sample of it to Pete.

'No water,' he cried. 'It's oil!' He was so excited he was shaking. He was drenched in oil and he drew his hand across his mouth as if making a meal of it. 'It's the real McCoy!'

Rachelle met Sarah dashing from her room. 'What's happened?' she demanded. 'Not another accident, please!'

Rachelle gave a pale smile. 'There's been an oil strike. Just as we were starting to eat.'

'There has?' Sarah hugged her in her delight. 'That's wonderful! I'm getting dressed and coming with you.'

The next hour or so was sheer pandemonium, and it was Sarah who struck the first note of sanity by drawing Rachelle on one side and saying, 'We'd better go back to the house to see what we can salvage from the meal. Pete isn't going to bed hungry.'

At last the uproar subsided. The men had ambled towards the kitchens on the site and were drowning their enthusiasm in drinks all round. Pete and Nancy had returned, had washed and changed, and Sarah had champagne on ice.

Toasts were drunk and they began to eat. For most of the time Rachelle avoided Pete's gaze. She had caught him looking at her intently from time to time, but his deep pleasant voice was not once directed at her.

Nancy was bubbling with laughter and was tossing down the champagne with a wicked chuckle. Pete had drawn up a place for Sarah at the table and had taken away the used dishes after each course to the kitchen.

Sarah protested that she had not actually strained her ankle and it was quite all right, but he had his way.

Rachelle felt too choked to eat. While she was glad that Pete's hard work had been rewarded, she knew that the gush of oil from the bowels of the earth had sprung up between them as unpenetrable as a brick wall.

Impossible to tell him now that she loved him, especially with Nancy's recently voiced insinuations that all she was interested in was the money from Pete's success.

Pete had followed Sarah to the kitchen to carry the coffee in and Rachelle with Nancy had left the table to seek the more comfortable chairs in the lounge when another sound erupted, this time more deadly.

There was the sound of shouting followed by the loud report of a gun reverberating on the night air. A second shot, and Jake burst into the lounge from the veranda window after shooting at the lock.

Both girls were on their feet and backing in horror.

Nancy said in a hoarse whisper, 'He's dead drunk!'

'You bet I am!'

Jake stood just inside the room, his eyes bloodshot, his speech slurred. The revolver in his hand was pointing at no one in particular, for he was dazed a little by the lighted room.

The next moment Rachelle was grabbed from behind and deposited on the other side of the lounge door.

Pete said urgently, 'Go quickly to your room and stay there. Understand?'

Did she feel his lips on her hair? Rachelle was not sure what happened in those split seconds, but she kept a clear head. Swiftly she made her way out of the bungalow and round to the front to creep on to the veranda.

The scene which met her eyes could well have been played in some movie. Pete had apparently snatched Nancy and had been about to push her from the room

to safety when Jake had protested, and demanded that
she should stay. Rachelle shivered. The air reeked of
oil. A faint hint of blueness hung on the night air.
There was broken glass on the lounge carpet from the
window through which Jake had forced an entry.

Pete stood erect and formidable in his anger with
Nancy pushed to one side almost behind him for protection. Rachelle was shaking all over, for Jake had
moved further into the room and was brandishing the
gun ominously in Nancy's direction.

'Oh, God!' Rachelle prayed silently. 'Please don't
let him shoot Pete. Please!'

Pete was facing the menace of the gun, his dark face
intent and ready to do murder himself.

'Put down that gun, you fool,' he snapped. 'If this is
a joke then I advise you to end it before I break your
neck!'

Rachelle's blue eyes were glued on Jake's profile. He
looked sick and desperately unhappy. He gestured with
the gun for Pete to move aside from Nancy, but Pete
replied by putting the girl right behind him.

'I'm warning you,' Pete growled, 'one shot from that
gun and I'll be on you before you can shoot a second.
Put it down and don't be a fool.'

Jake mumbled indistinctly, 'I'll be more of a fool if
I do.' He swayed on his feet. 'I'm ... talking to you,
Nancy,' he went on. 'The game ish ... up.'

The last word came from his lips in the form of a
hiccup. A drunken man was not responsible for his
actions, Rachelle thought distractedly, and cupped her
face with shaking hands. If Pete died she wanted to die
too.

Pete said more quietly, 'What game are you talking
about?'

Jake waved the gun to his side. 'Her. Ask her.'

Nancy came out from behind Pete. 'You're drunk, Jake. You don't know what you're talking about,' she said brazenly.

Jake seemed to sober up for a minute. He sneered, 'Is that why you've lost colour?' He gestured with his head towards Pete. 'Why don't you tell him he's handling secondhand goods where you're concerned? Does he knew about our little affair before you met him?'

Nancy's mouth went tight, and a slight flush stained her cheeks. Her red hair seemed on fire, her tawny eyes like those of a cat with claws.

'Oh, come now, Jake, you're jumping to conclusions. Can't we discuss this like rational beings? Put the gun down, for goodness' sake. You don't want to land yourself in jail just as you've struck oil. Why, you're going to be rich!'

Nancy's voice was quite steady, her tones a musical purr. To Rachelle, transfixed on the veranda, the slight movement she made forward towards Jake was feline.

Pete, tall and stern, waiting for a chance to close in, said, 'Nancy's right. Let's discuss whatever is bothering you.'

Jake turned to point the gun menacingly at Pete and Rachelle quelled a scream.

'You keep out of this,' he warned. 'This is between Nancy and me.'

Nancy avoided Pete's restraining hand and moved forward slinkily.

'All right, Jake. But let's talk sensibly. You're going to feel a complete idiot in the morning.'

Jake was staring at Nancy like someone in a trance.

In her green dress with its low neckline, her shoulders gleamed softly in the light, her full lips pouted invitingly.

Rachelle could well imagine the effect she had on Jake. Poor Jake, she thought. He loves her. Rachelle was saying inwardly, she wants a man, Jake, someone who will show her who's master. You can do it. Had she whispered the words aloud? Pete could not have heard them, he was too far away. Had Nancy? Before she could be sure Jake had taken Nancy's wrist in his strong hand.

'We're having no more nonsense,' he told her. 'You promised to marry me if we made a strike, and you're going to do just that, so help me.'

'Of course I am,' Nancy purred, 'you silly boy!'

For answer Jake caught her savagely in his arms and crushed her to him. The gun fell unheeded to the floor and Rachelle did not wait to see the look on Pete's face.

In the kitchen Sarah was sitting at the table staring unseeingly at the coffee percolator.

'What's happened?' she cried as Rachelle walked in. 'I thought it best to do nothing and leave it to Pete. Jake is well and truly drunk and anything could happen.'

'It has,' Rachelle said weakly, leaning against the kitchen table. 'Jake and Nancy are in a clinch and Nancy seems to be enjoying it. Anyway, Jake's dropped the gun.'

Sarah gave a sigh of relief. 'Thank heaven for that! I knew Pete could handle it. I told you that girl would bring trouble. Are you all right? You look very pale.'

Rachelle nodded. 'Did you know Nancy had an affair with Jake once?'

Sarah shrugged. 'Show me any man around who she

hasn't had an affair with. I'll make a drink—we all need one. You look dead on your feet. Sit down.'

Rachelle pushed the bright hair back from her damp forehead, feeling peculiar. In a voice hardly recognisable as her own she said feebly, 'I'll take a peep in the lounge to see how things are going.'

She made her way to the bathroom first, feeling very sick. But nothing happened as she leaned over the wash basin and dabbed her forehead with cold water. After a while she went to the lounge and peeped in. All was quiet. Pete sat alone. He was hunched forward holding his head in his hands.

Rachelle felt her heart bursting with love for him, but pride held her back. What could she do? He was obviously shattered because Nancy had gone with Jake. Besides, if she told him that she wanted to stay with him he would think it was because he had struck oil.

Slowly she dragged herself back to the kitchen where Sarah was loading the freshly made coffee and cups on a tray.

With pale lips, she said, 'Pete is all alone. I didn't stay because he looks all in. I am too. Will you tell him I'll see him in the morning? I'm off to bed.'

'But surely you're having a drink first? Pete will probably go back to the workings right away.'

Rachelle shook her head. 'No, thanks.' She managed a smile. 'Didn't have much of a rest, did you? How's the ankle?'

Sarah laughed. 'Do you know, I'd forgotten all about it! That shows how bad it was.'

Rachelle kissed her cheek affectionately. 'You're a darling, Sarah. I don't know what we would have done without you.'

She stood with her back against the bedroom door, disregarding her weariness, trying to think what she must do. She was just a fool of a girl so much in love with her husband that she did not care what kind of a job he had as long as she was with him. But it was too late. And he would never know. Slackly she began to fold up her clothes and pack them into her suitcase.

CHAPTER TEN

RACHELLE went in to breakfast feeling unrefreshed after a sleepless night.

Sarah told her, 'We have a visitor, so breakfast is in the dining room this morning.'

Rachelle was off in a flash before Sarah had finished speaking, to teeter on the threshold of the room as a well dressed figure turned from the window to greet her.

'Tony!' she cried in astonished surprise. 'How nice to see you. What are you doing in this part of the world?'

He took her hands in his and grinned. 'Congratulations. I bet you're over the moon about Pete's success. Were you expecting someone else?'

Rachelle laughed. 'To tell you the truth I thought Grandpa had come with his new wife. How are you?'

She drew him to the breakfast table and they sat down.

'You haven't told me what you're doing here,' she reminded him as Sarah came in with a tray.

Tony waited until Sarah had left the room, then he said soberly,

'You're still of the same mind in wanting to join my project ... I mean, you haven't changed your mind since Pete's windfall?'

She said quietly, 'Is that why you're here?'

'Goodness, no. I could hardly have come so quickly, could I? As a matter of fact Pete sent for me a few days ago.'

'I see.' Rachelle lifted her fruit juice to her lips with cold fingers and drank. 'Did he say why he was sending for you?' she added, putting down her glass.

He shook his head. 'No. Could be he was anticipating something would happen. I lent him money for extra equipment for the oil drilling based on an idea of his and it paid off. I'm very glad for him.'

'Yes, it's wonderful news, but I'm still going on with my career.' Rachelle wished her voice did not sound so wobbly. 'As a matter of fact,' she added on a note of bravado, 'you couldn't have come at a better time. My bags are already packed.'

Tony smiled. 'Have you arranged a flight back?'

She shook her head, unable to speak. What on earth was the matter with her? Everything was going her way. Tony would take her back with him and that was that. He was saying,

'Good. I shall arrange that you go back with me. It should be easy enough.'

He went on to talk about the progress being made on the buildings for his art centre. She would like her flat, with all the latest gadgets and the wonderful views from the windows.

Breakfast was over when Rachelle had the courage to ask about Pete.

'I don't know where he is,' Tony answered. 'He drove me here, then said he would leave us to settle things on our own. I'm going to stroll down to the location later. We can leave this evening if you like. No point in staying, is there?'

Rachelle agreed. She wanted no long-drawn-out goodbyes. Soon she would be gone without knowing if Nancy and Jake were going to marry. If it was a trick on Nancy's part to calm Jake down with a lie and go back to Pete, Rachelle did not want to know.

When Tony had gone out she stood on the veranda for a while looking towards the creek. At least there was a part of herself there. It was her place of refuge. It was also the solid reminder of things she wanted to forget; those times swimming in the clear spring water with Pete.

Dejectedly, Rachelle turned her footsteps towards it for the last time. Pete had made the first move in severing their relationship by sending for Tony Spelling. He obviously could not wait to be rid of her. The trouble was that she had never trusted her love for him. She had never truly given him anything. Her vision had been warped by material things, home comforts before she had earned them.

True love meant trusting your man and letting that trust inspired by your love uplift you in your struggles together. She was nearing the creek and lifting her face to the dappled reflection of green foliage. There was the fresh smell of grass and water. Rachelle breathed in deeply and lowered her eyes, then she froze. Pete sat in their favourite spot, knees drawn up, looking into the water.

It was too late for her to retreat, for he turned his head slowly and looked at her calmly. Their gazes held, bleak with emptiness ... Rachelle backed a little, feeling the spell of his presence, finding him so heartbreakingly dear and as wonderful as when they had bathed together in this very creek, to lie afterwards kissing with the scent of crushed grass giving magic to their love with heaven very near.

The long quivering breath came from her heart. Her voice was a husky whisper.

'I'm sorry about Nancy. Is she really going to marry Jake?'

His dark face was expressionless. 'I guess so.'

He rose slowly to his feet as if every muscle in his body ached intolerably and thrust his hands into his pockets. Rachelle longed to reach up to caress his lean dark face ... to utter words of comfort. Never had she known such aching misery.

Tears pricked her eyes, but all the tears in the world could not help her now. Pete had shown so plainly that he did not want her by sending for Tony Spelling to take her away. For the rest of her life she would regret what might have been.

So much she would always remember, the dark springy hair, the grey eyes tender and mocking, the clear-cut mouth in all its moods, the bronze satin of his skin gleaming with drops of water from the creek, those strong hands caressing her tenderly; his arms close around her, his hard body against her soft yielding one, his kisses.

Rachelle found her voice. 'Why did you send for Tony Spelling?'

He lifted a dark brow. 'You ask me that? You're going back with him?'

The words were more of a statement than a question. They hurt intolerably. Anger gave her a controlled, calm strength with the urge to creep away to some corner and lick her wounds like some wounded animal. Pete was giving her no choice. He had never intended to.

'There was never any doubt about it, was there?'

The words fell from her lips without her being aware of having spoken them.

He said, 'I'll walk back with you to the house. What time are you leaving?'

'This evening. Tony thinks there'll be little difficulty in getting me a flight back with him.'

Neither of them spoke again in the short walk back. They were met by Tony.

'I've been looking for you, Pete,' he said. 'You're wanted down on the field.'

As Pete strode away Tony looked at Rachelle's pale face. His voice was filled with concern.

'Are you all right, dear?' he asked, taking her arm. 'You haven't much colour.'

'The excitement,' she replied. 'I ... I can't believe it. I think I'll rest for a while and take it all in—if you don't mind?'

He gave her arm a fatherly pat. 'Not at all. Actually, I was going back to the field with Pete. See you later.'

Rachelle had got as far as the lounge when Sarah called from the kitchen.

'Nancy is here to see you. I'm going out for vegetables from the garden.'

Before Rachelle could move further Nancy stood in the doorway looking at her, a subdued Nancy but with a kind of tranquillity about her that somehow made her a stranger.

She spoke without the usual preliminaries. 'I'm going to marry Jake. I thought you'd like to know.'

Rachelle could not even smile. 'Congratulations. Pete told me.'

Nancy bit her lip. 'So you've made it up?'

Rachelle shook her head. 'I fail to see what business it is of yours, but no, we haven't. I'm leaving this evening.'

For a moment Nancy was taken aback. Then her lip curled. The amber eyes were filled with scorn.

'So you can't take it, after all,' she sneered.

'Take what? Pete's dream of striking oil has come true. From now on it will be plain sailing—or should I say luxurious sailing?—for you all.'

Nancy said coldly, 'What I told you about the strike being barely enough to cover expenses still stands as yet. May I suggest that as a token of good will you give your shares in the company to Pete. They'll help enormously if he has to sell out. Goodbye, Rachelle. Pleasant journey.'

Rachelle stood for a long time where Nancy had left her before stumbling to her room. Dislike of Nancy and all she stood for gradually melted away on a wave of despair that left her numb. What Nancy had told her about the oil strike made no difference because there was still doubt as to how big a strike it was.

She would leave her shares to Pete. If only the strike had come after she had told him how much she loved him, that she would follow him barefoot if need be across the world.

It was quite an effort to sit down and write him a letter telling him that the shares were his. Tears kept falling on the page and she had to use endless sheets of paper, but at last it was done. Steeped in the depths of remorse, Rachelle put the letter in an envelope and propped it up on her dressing table. Pete would find it when she had gone.

After that Rachelle moved round in a dream, making sure that everything was packed. Stony-faced, she did all the usual things and cleaned the room. This time she was sure no ghosts of Rachelle Standring would be left behind. She heard Sarah cleaning Pete's room. Later, hearing her in the bathroom, Rachelle went along to Pete's room.

There she fondled his hairbrushes and put the dressing robe against her cheek. Inhaling his after-shave, Rachelle knew it would be the nearest she would ever get to him. It was then that she saw the signed photograph of Nancy on the dressing table, and sparks of anger glittered in her eyes. If she was to leave no ghosts of herself neither was Nancy!

With one violent movement the picture was beneath her feet and she was trampling on it viciously.

'What the hell is going on?'

Rachelle stopped dead in her tracks to gaze in horror at Pete, who had come in from the bathroom with a towel around his waist. He reached for his wrap and shrugged into it, tying the cord.

Rachelle quivered. There was a breaking point, and she had reached it.

'It's Nancy's picture ... I ... smashed it.'

She was shaking all over as Pete bent down to pick up the smashed picture.

He looked startled. 'Where did this come from?' he demanded.

'From ... from your ... dressing table. Where else?'

His mouth thinned. 'I've never seen this picture before.'

They stared at each other for a long moment while

Pete dropped the mangled photograph into the waste paper basket. He had never taken his dark grey eyes from her accusing ones. The physical proof of how much they loved each other was in their eyes.

An endearing smile lifted the corners of his mouth as he held out his arms.

'I love you, Pete,' she sobbed as his arms closed around her. 'I hope it's true what Nancy says, that the oil strike isn't what you hoped it would be. I want to cook and clean for you, to look after you. I don't want to go away.'

The fragrance of her silky hair was soft against his lips, the salt of her tears. He was kissing her mouth, her soft throat, crushing her suppleness against him. His lips found hers again and they stood locked in each other's arms, savouring exquisite long minutes of ecstatic reunion.

At last Pete released her enough to look down into her glowing face.

'Nice to have you back again, darling,' he said. 'Only this time it's for keeps. I'll never let you go again.'

Her eyes were wide blue pools of glistening tears. 'You really love me? I haven't killed your love by being such a fool?'

Ardent moments passed as he answered in the only way. He laughed softly as she clung to him, close and fiercely loving. Then he sobered, and guided her to sit beside him on the bed.

'I think I'd better qualify my last remark,' he said with an arm around her. 'It's not going to be easy. I want children and they'll come naturally, not when we decide we can afford them. They'll be born out of our love for each other and not according to our budget. Think you can stand it?—because I don't want to go through the last months without you ever again.'

Rachelle kissed the powerful chest visible between the lapels of his dressing gown and said huskily, 'Just try to get rid of me, that's all. I'll trail around after you, children and all.'

Her lips moved upwards. The bliss of being able to kiss his firm brown throat again, to know that he loved her as she loved him!

'Do you love Nancy, Pete?' she asked tremulously.

'Of course I love her. We all do. Men are more tolerant than women regarding their sex. She's a real live pin-up for the boys, much better than a picture in a paper. I've never made love to her, though. She's been here this morning, hasn't she, and left her picture in my room. I wonder why?'

'Perhaps because I told her that you and I hadn't made up our differences. Maybe she thought her picture would be company for you,' Rachelle said generously. 'I wish I hadn't destroyed it now. I'm sorry.' She kissed his chin. 'I was jealous because I was sure you loved her. When Nancy and Jake had gone after the shooting you sat alone in the lounge looking like a man who'd lost everything—including Nancy.'

He lifted her chin and kissed her. 'Do you know why I sat like that? I'd never felt so shattered in my life. Do you realise that Jake might have killed you? That's why I threw you out of the room quick. He was dead drunk. One slip of his trigger finger, and you ...'

He broke off to seize her in his arms and whisper against her lips, thickly.

'I love you more than life itself and I'll always have nightmares about that shooting. I've been driven to distraction thinking I'd lose you—that's why I said unforgivable things to you. We have a lot to make up for, my sweet wife.'

Ardent moments passed as he proceeded to make up for lost time telling her how he loved her. The sudden rap on the door brought them back to earth.

'Don't you two want any lunch?' called Sarah outside their door. 'And don't forget you have a guest, will you?'

'Tony!' they cried, convulsed.

That night when Tony Spelling had gone, leaving them with his good wishes ringing in their ears, Rachelle sat up in bed waiting for Pete to come in from the bathroom. When he came she handed him the letter giving him her shares in the company.

'What's this?' he asked as he shed his robe and slid into bed beside her.

'I thought it would help,' she told him modestly.

He scanned the letter, put it down on the bedside table and slid down into the bed to take her in his arms.

'I'd better tell you that I shall have enough money to buy cattle and start the ranch I've always dreamed about. Mind you, we shall have to make it pay. The only help I shall accept from my parents is their experience.'

He pushed the silky hair back from her face and kissed her.

'We shan't be well off for a long, long time because the profits will have to be ploughed back into the ranch. So if you want to back out now's the time. You see, darling,' he whispered against her lips, 'after tonight I can't guarantee that you'll be free to go as you came.'

Rachelle's face went hot at the implication of his words.

'Darling,' she said on a chuckle, 'do you think your

parents will object to a miniature Pete strutting around the place after the trouble they've had with you?'

He groaned. 'They'll be over the moon about it, but he's going to be terribly spoiled.'

'Then we shall have to make sure there are others to cut him down to size, won't we?' she whispered.

Pete's answer was to draw her to him and, as Rachelle gave him her lips, she knew she just could not wait for the rest of her dreams to come true. Pete was hers for life and this was only the beginning.